Penguin Books
Penguin Modern Stories 1

Penguin
Modern
Stories 1

Edited by Judith Burnley

Penguin Books

Penguin Books Ltd, Harmondsworth,
Middlesex, England
Penguin Books Inc., 7110 Ambassador Road,
Baltimore, Maryland 21207, U.S.A.
Penguin Books Australia Ltd, Ringwood,
Victoria, Australia

First published in book form in Great Britain by
Penguin Books Ltd 1969
Reprinted 1969

Made and printed in Great Britain by
Cox & Wyman Ltd, London, Reading and Fakenham
Set in Intertype Baskerville

Contents

Introduction

There are today so few serious publications devoted to the short story that there is no need, in introducing *Penguin Modern Stories,* to say more than that we believe in the short story, know that a great many of the best contemporary writers are working in this form, and look forward to publishing many well-known authors as well as introducing many new ones. All these stories are published here for the first time in this country.

William Sansom

Down at the Hydro

As Colonel Hunt awoke – and it must have been the sound of the door bursting open which woke him – he was conscious of a huge figure in hussar's dark dolman and white busby bearing fast across the room at him, pointing at his face something that glinted dangerously ... and for that hairsbreadth second he lay dead still, alerted, assessing the danger but forgetting where he was or what campaign or country or how such a uniform ... Moravia? Slovenia? ... before with a mighty lurch he flung himself sideways across the bed and stopped just in time from crashing to the floor and upsetting his morning glass of hot water in the nurse's hand.

'Dreams?' the nurse sang at him, as crisp morning air came in behind her high starched bonnet and short blue cloak. 'Well you can't blame the roast duck and lobster sauce, can you, Colonel?'

'Morning, nurse,' the Colonel grunted, and took his allotted glass and the plate of sliced orange. 'Fat lot of duck we see here. What's for lunch?'

'Yoghurt and honey,' the nurse said, 'like everyone else.'

'Nevertheless it's a lovely day again, I see. Beautiful weather for October.'

'Blanket bath at ten. The chiropractor'll want you for ten minutes at twelve-fifteen. Right?'

The nurse ticked a list, smiled and withdrew. The Colonel settled himself comfortably back on big white pillows and

9

sipped his water, keeping the orange till last, while the eight o'clock sun sent long morning shadows over a lawn grey with dew.

'Like hoar frost', he thought, 'quite extraordinary,' as he looked out through the little lattice window and noticed with further surprise two squirrels racing batlike down the wide grey trunk of a beech. The squirrels then began a furry-tailed game beneath the tree. The Colonel drew in a deep breath of the pine-scented fresh air, and felt, as so many do at the blessing of fair weather, how very good it was to be alive.

Especially after that foray with the hussar? No, there was something else specially good about the morning. What? . . . But of course . . . two huts away lay that handsome little Mrs Mackay, who had smiled so charmingly at him yesterday. A collusive smile, as if there was understanding between them. For it had been a smile at the expense of others.

Colonel Hunt was installed for a hungry week in one of the gazebos at Elm Park, a dietary hydro in Wiltshire. The gazebos, a row of a dozen comfortable summer-houses, were set along the lawn edge. They stood separate from the main building, and in them one could enjoy not only a direct contact with nature but also the comforts of a miniature nursing home – warm soft white bed, cream walls, running water, a chinzy armchair, a kidney-shaped dressing-table, a low-toned bedside wireless in brown bakelite. Each gazebo also boasted cottagey little valanced curtains, a bronze-painted wicker chair, an electric blanket and an electric fire: there was television, too, if you wanted it. Many of those who occupied a gazebo felt, after a few days, a kind of fury against their own spacious houses or flats, income-eaters, foot-sorers, fabrications of worry and dirt – for here, almost within arm's length, lay everything one person could possibly wish for. Lavatories and bathrooms stood close behind in a laurel thicket, and there was all the lawn for a stretch of the legs. Healthily selfish minds soon realized that their damnable homes were designed not for them but for other people; or for their possessions which, as always, possessed them. A few rigorously selfless people congratulated themselves on the same score.

So – a bedsitter *au natur*! A service flatlet *camping*! The Colonel had seen the instant good sense of it, and now swore to give up his house and buy a caravan. He would buy a permanent field, rove England for holidays as the weather dictated, and this would save him the further bother of all these travel brochures . . . he daydreamed on, a flexible mind in a stiffening body . . . on balance, he loathed as much as loved the house which the laws of acquisition had told him to love; he liked what he had done to it, and the sight of a few trophies and pictures, but lived and paced alone in it. His wife, not he, had been killed by high explosive in Cyprus years before, a turn of fate which still bewildered him, and now in the early sixties, beset by those feelings of physical tiredness which result in their opposite, in a last access before it is too late of action, he wanted deeply to throw up everything and make a change. It was also why, as a gesture, he had chosen to try for the first time a week of enemas and starvation: a purging and a renewal. It was also why his thoughts quickened towards Mrs Mackay.

Mrs Mackay lay in her own gazebo and listened to an electric organ play a humoresque. Fifty-five, she had thought on waking, and lay there longing for the days of fifty-four and three, so much further removed from sixty. Though thus a victim of the decimal system, she had triumphed well over time itself. She could pass for forty in a shady room, a clever dark rinse kept out the grey, and her health was good apart from a hardening roll above her suspender belt. But only she – and perhaps her husband – knew of this. Its correction was the cause of her presence at Elm Park.

The humoresque cossetted her. Awful Palm Court stuff, she thought, but gave in and listened to its soothing tinkle of security. Like the sunny cream walls, like the chintzes, it took her back to the simpler thirties, when the children were children and they had all lived and laughed together in an ample gabled house in Surrey. Life then had seemed to have a future. Fir trees in the garden, mudguards glinting on the gravel drive, tradesmen at their entrance, a cook in the kitchen ... well, now it was a three-roomer in Kensington, the war survived, the children dispersed, the Change done with. One continued to dress oneself, play bridge and see friends and so on ... but none of it had the same sense of purpose.

So it was pleasant to dream backwards and lie in such a gazebo as this, well looked after by a white-aproned staff, reminiscent autumn sunlight shining through the windows, and not a sign about the room of the changed years. The television somehow fitted in, one could not now imagine life without it. Even those voices outside, which yesterday had occasioned her mutual smile with Colonel Hunt, matched the mood. They were loud, educated, shingle-beach voices of women called Hazel and Phyllis who called to each other constantly by name, who began a conversation at the tops of their voices fifty yards apart, absolutely unaffected by the garden quiet or by the presence of anyone else. Such voices, ringing out across beaches or tennis courts or packed buses, had an enviable surety. At first they sounded simply thick-skinned, but they also bore the booming message that all was well with the world, the Stock Exchange and Mummy. Ha-azel! ... Phy-llis! Once, with Hazel hidden within her gazebo, Phyllis had really carolled out 'Coo-ee' as she came trudging across the turf in her flowered peignoir – and it was then that Mrs Mackay had caught the Colonel's eye.

A handsome old chap, she had thought, and found herself wondering how he would have been as a husband: for it was strange indeed, they both sitting quite close on deckchairs in dressing-gowns and night-clothes, as if on some connubial lawn. She was glad he had a sense of humour. They were allies! It would be nice to have someone to chat to. There was a week to go. And then she caught sight of the squirrels, and her thoughts turned guiltily to the hollow trunk of her secret oak tree away at the thicket end of the garden. All alone she blushed.

A Mrs Davidson, in her gazebo to the left of the Colonel's, awoke abruptly with the single thought: 'Long-chairs!' Even before tasting her hot water, she was into her dressing-gown and off to the main building, where, stacked in a loggia among simple deckchairs, four or five expensive garden-chairs with arms and canopies glittered their chromium. Mrs Davidson abstracted one and hurried back with it to her gazebo. 'And that's cooked *their* goose,' she muttered before returning to bed, water and wireless.

'Ha-azel!' came the hunter's call dying far off in the woods, 'Ha-aze!' – startling the squirrels – 'I've got my colo-o-nic at eleven.'

Silence, as the squirrels ran up the tree.

'Hazel! Aren't you *awake* yet?'

Colonel Hunt and Mrs Mackay smiled together in their separate beds. Both reached for their dressing-gowns. The morning had begun.

Phyllis's flowered rump was disappearing into Hazel's gazebo as the Colonel and Mrs Hunt issued from theirs. They smiled at each other and the Colonel put his hand across his mouth in mock laughter as Mrs Mackay came walking towards him.

'Morning,' he said. 'Lovely morning. You just off to the torture chamber?' Then abruptly he looked down at his slippered feet and fled inside again, muttering 'Excuse me'.

He had, of course, meant the main building with its massage beds and sitz baths, its irrigation machines and sweating blankets. But the same path led round to the lavatories! Almighty Heavens, how ghastly ... poor woman, he thought ... and from behind a curtain observed Mrs Mackay in fact proceed round and into the laurels: for now, with the Colonel so surprisingly disappeared, she had nothing better to do.

Later Colonel Hunt lay bound up in hot blankets and sweated doubly to think of how churlish he must have seemed – if not for his statement, then certainly for his sudden exit. Powerless he lay and watched the clock, and decided the more powerfully to put everything right later with an all-out invitation to take an afternoon walk together.

He met her again, mid-morning, in the corridor, on her way to be massaged, and quite abruptly – for he was a man of decision – put the matter to her.

'Why, that would be lovely,' she said. 'After tea?'

'After tea,' he smiled, and added, to make matters quite clear, 'Blanket bath this morning. Torture's the word, no mistake.'

She had hardly noticed his earlier phrase, and now wondered whether perhaps he was not inclined to be a trifle garrulous.

After collecting his yoghurt and honey from the Sun Room, and after an afternoon nap in bed and then tea alone in his gazebo – the restaurant reminded him too much of residential hotels for the lonely – the Colonel dressed, heard her voice somewhere outside, and hurried his tie along.

She was speaking to a woman stretched on a luxurious garden-chair set on the lawn.

'They're so *selfish*,' this woman was saying, as he came up. 'They get these long-chairs and set them out with their knitting and books and then go in for their treatments!'

She pronounced 'long-chairs' as one word, accenting the adjective, making it thus cosier – like those who seem to produce a new household category when they say: 'I do like a good-book.'

'Too bad,' said Mrs Mackay.

'So I said to myself, I said two can play at that game. I got up good and early and nabbed one and brought it here.'

'Haha,' said Mrs Mackay. Then, 'But aren't you also being a bit . . . you know?'

'A bit what?' asked Mrs Davidson. It was a rhetorical question. For she went on repeating: 'Selfish, utterly selfish.'

Once again the Colonel met Mrs Mackay's eyes, now over this Mrs Davidson's canopy. Again they smiled in conspiracy. And together made their excuses and set off on their walk.

'Don't you go having any buttered toast teas in the village,' Mrs Davidson gaily called after them. 'My God, I could do with a steak and chips.'

They waved, and again privately grimaced to each other. This was a very ordinary brand of Elm Park humour among the starving rich, most of whom joked about food from morning till dusk.

Alone together it was a little difficult at first. Dressed, they felt like strangers. But as soon as they left the garden for the pine woods and browning bracken, there followed an easy enough interchange, the simple pleasantries of two people finding out about each other. In spite of, or because of, three days' starvation, they both felt energetic and set off at a good pace.

The Colonel looked down and approved of her sensible tweeds. And Mrs Mackay also benefited from one of the few natural kindnesses of increasing age: for the Colonel's ageing eyes, without his reading glasses, automatically ironed out any wrinkles in her daylit face. Pretty little woman, he thought, and with such a sense of fun.

From time to time she glanced up at him and thought he had a charming smile, boyish almost – a sudden show of teeth under a moustache often has this effect – but more than that she liked the kindly interest in his eyes, and his overall manly, decided presence. How absurd, she thought, this old idea of 'the peppery Colonel'! This man was full of humour, and understanding, and seemed alive to so much. Quite rightly, it occurred to her that this might be due to a lifetime spent in studying the men under him, and coming up against all sorts of passing practical problems. Pepper was out-dated. Discipline and regulations were only a useful armour covering an immense disorder of human problems.

He pointed out to her a small Victorian house isolated in the bracken: cream-washed façade, apple-green paint, polished brass – traditional Victorian Country Council colours, he said. Anything from a verger's residence to a lock-keeper's cottage, you can always tell: probably a Council's wood-ranger, in this case. Apple-green, he said – not institutional dark green as in London. Then he told her how squirrels, pretty little nut-fanciers, attacked and ate any small animal they could find. Store up the wounded bird for Christmas, he joked: and politely apologized. He told her that Elm Park with its turrets and battlements had been built originally for a rich tea merchant, and conjured up visions of stirring days when the place shone green with gaslight. And so on – he hated pockets, wished men carried handbags. And his masseur played the drums, of all things, as a hobby. *Bongos*, he said.

Mrs Mackay was not particularly interested in any of these remarks, preferring talk of persons rather than things, but she was in a mood to hang on his words whatever they were; and indeed she wondered at the roving, inquiring nature of his mind. Especially about the handbags – so strange in a military man. But of course, they carried knapsacks and things? Hazily she saw herself walking up the Brompton Road with a neat khaki waterbottle full of gin and orange bouncing against her thigh.

The bracken smelled peppery, woodsmoke from a bonfire rose like a calm blue pillar on the windless air, a pleasant chill seemed to make everything more silent. Delightful smells of rot hung wetly about. Their voices echoed. And then an extraordinary thing happened. A man in rough clothes came along the path towards them and, as they passed, touched the Colonel's arm.

'Pardon, Guv ... got the price of a cup o' tea? I've not took a bite of food for two whole days ...'

The Colonel could not help himself, he simply doubled over. Mrs Mackay did not know where to look.

Then Colonel Hunt straightened up, looking gravely concerned. 'I'm sorry,' he said to the man, 'a sudden – er – twinge – ' and he added, 'Here,' searching his pockets.

But at Elm Park nobody carried money, there was no need. The Colonel looked wildly at Mrs Mackay, who simply spread her hands, unable to trust herself to speak. The man stood waiting. At last the Colonel said to the man: 'I'm afraid I've not a penny on me.' And then he took out his tobacco pouch: 'Here, take this. It's good for a bob or two.'

'Oh no, sir, I couldn't.'

'Go on, man!'

'Thank you, sir, but no. Very kind of you, I'm sure.'

And on he went up the path without another word.

The Colonel muttered, 'My heavens, I've never been so embarrassed in all my life.' And repeated it again later two or three times when they were on the way home. She was touched both by his offer of so very personal a thing as the tobacco pouch, and by how truly upset he seemed to be.

'Still, it'll make a good story!' she laughed.

'I thought I'd burst,' he said. 'But it's worn pretty thin now.'

The episode brought them closer; and so, even more, did Mrs Davidson meeting them on their return.

'I went inside for three minutes,' she howled at them, '*three* minutes, and my long-chair was gone!'

The next morning, Colonel Hunt showed up for the first time for PT on the terrace. He knew he could still cut a pretty good figure. Mrs Mackay, for opposite reasons, for the first time stayed away.

To soft cooing of the instructor, the Colonel went through the appropriate actions and wondered at himself. At his age? And knowing quite well that the lady was married? Still ... a minor flirtation, what harm was there? Besides, why call it a flirtation – it was more an attractive

17

companionship. But he knew he was far too much excited. And he was not used to it. The sun slanted down on another lovely day, the sky spread its wide distant blue, and Colonel Hunt thrust out his arms right and left to punish himself.

The yellow brick and slate towers of Elm Park rose in state alongside the exercise terrace. What strange mutations lay behind its stately façade! What irony within the treatment rooms, those white clinical bowels where once wine cellars, larders and kitchens had confected their poisonous opposite, vast and liverish Victorian banquets! Already the 'fast' had lost Colonel Hunt several pounds in weight, and had made him feel years younger. It worked! For the idea of this starvation and colonic cleansing was not only to reduce fat but also to search out deep and secretive poisons never otherwise expunged. In one of the textbooks supplied with his gazebo, he had read, among run-of-the-mill case histories, of more extreme events, particularly one of a woman who was seriously ill, and who had fasted for three weeks, and whose gall bladder, on the twenty-first day, had suddenly 'yielded up' no less than 'fifty-three tiny gallstones'. If this could happen, what other changes might not come over a physique enfevered by regained energy, lost fat, dropped years? One had better look out.

They met again in the Sun Lounge for lunch.

The luncheon hour was a kind of social parade, when everyone gathered in assorted dressing-gowns, house-coats, peignoirs, kimonos or négligés, according to their place in fashionable history. One was put in mind of an oddly pale-faced assembly of robed West African diplomats. A colourful assembly indeed and in the sunny orange-painted room brightly overspirited, for it was one of the big moments of what was jokingly called 'a full day'. No one wished to appear put out by the lack of food: everyone rattled their apple-plates and yoghurt spoons and talked at the tops of their voices. Innocent of alcohol, they all looked very tipsy. It was thus like a cocktail party: and with the eerie look of a cocktail party in a film, no smoke and glassily clear.

The Colonel observed on this to Mrs Mackay. 'With the usual empty chatter,' he added.

'Colonel!' frowned Mrs Mackay, choking on honey and a mousse of gooseberries.

Quite a crowd. Altogether some forty or fifty people came and went or sat about on the wall-seats. Occasionally, gusted on a moment's pause, the voices of Hazel and Phyllis came ringing across the room. 'Five pounds lost in five days – *that's* little me!' 'Little's not the word, Haze. Yours truly's got into a girdle bought in the year *one*!'

But nearer to the Colonel and Mrs Mackay, at a large table and somehow domineering all others, sat a group of three richly clad women and their men, the men in very silk pyjamas and the women halo-ed by wildly ruched négligés. Pink and blonded, these women looked like large and expensive powder-puffs. All had firm Lancashire accents. Glinting with gold and jewellery, lacquered hair, cosmetics, the women talked of champagne cocktails and swimming pools, while the men quietly costed the running of such a hydro. It would seem that they would run it twice as efficiently – adding a room for chemmy – and that the women on their return home would get blind drunk and drown in their pools. 'And, darling, roast beef and Yorkshire pud *hanging* over the sides of the plate!' They would sink to the bottom.

Next to these gilded and wealthy ones who, with their pools and long fast cars, their vast new electric kitchens, their overpaid Spanish servants and their curious successes in the tax battle, really enjoyed the amenities of our contemporary gadget-mad, tax-chess years – next to these the contemporary affluent sat a really rich man, quiet, sad, and deeply sunburned, who never even saw an income tax form. He did not know what he missed, encumbered as he was only with the dull burden of giving, always giving, and the duller one of having to live with and appear to like an invaluable art collection expected of him by society. His resignation was complete, he ate his yoghurt as slowly as if it were a five course meal; his eyes had the stoical sadness of the cheap Arab labour which worked his oil – exile in the Mediterranean had made him nearly as brown.

The Colonel pointed this man out to Mrs Mackay, who in turn pointed out a tiny actress in dark glasses hiding with her manager in a corner. Then they caught the eye of Mrs Davidson, who mouthed at them and jabbed an accusing finger towards the colourful group of affluent Lancastrians. Mrs Mackay smiled back, and whispered to the Colonel: 'I met her stretched out again this morning. She was talking of buying a padlock.'

Here and there it was to be noticed that inmates were already dressed in day clothes, suits or dresses. Treatment over for the day, they would drive into the local town to shop for antiques or go to the cinema, and often for darker reasons. It was said that the number of the town's tea-shops had trebled since Elm Park began operating. But nobody spoke of this. It was dangerous. Dr Joseff, doyen of the Hydro, had been known to require bun-dodging patients to leave on the very next day. And Dr Joseff was adamant. In spite of the Hydro's nickname – Slippery Joe's, after the Slippery Elm food included in the doctor's diet – Joseff was a man of severe vocation. Speaking of this man, and likening the bun-dodgers to secretaries and F.O. officials at this pale Nigerian spree – Mrs Mackay suddenly said: 'You know, I really can't be bothered to dress today. Couldn't we perhaps take a stroll just round the garden later on – I mean, it's huge really. That is, if you'd like to?'

The Colonel wondered at a certain strained nonchalance in her tone, but passed it over in his great pleasure. Their companionship was settled! and later that afternoon Mrs Mackay steered him across the lawns and by the last flower-beds into the dark moss-grown paths of a kind of wilderness thicket far from any view of the house.

Eventually, in an overhung place where a hollow, lightning-struck oak stood, she stopped and turned to him. 'I've – I've got a secret to tell you,' she began, and the Colonel felt his pulses quicken, both fearful and excited by such sudden intimacy. In that hidden, shadowy place.

She was looking up at him with eyes shining dangerously. 'I hope you won't think badly of me,' she whispered, 'but I . . . I . . .'

He bent towards her. His heart was beating hard, he felt it unchivalrous to let her bear all the initiative, and he began to murmur 'Mrs Mackay . . . Deirdre . . .' when her face abruptly receded, dropped away like a lift, and there she was bent down at his feet. What? No! But then he saw she was scrabbling a hand in a hole in the dead oak tree. Triumphantly she brought out a big coloured tin.

'Lemon curd tarts,' she whispered, 'walnut sponge, petit beurres and a couple of old sausage rolls!'

'Good Lord!' said Colonel Hunt.

'So now you know me for what I am!' she pouted. 'Banger, my lord?'

The Colonel took a sausage roll like one crucified. He was more put out by this breaking of rules than by the disappointment of his hopes, which had instantly been outplaced by the enormity of this new collusion. He liked the rules, he believed in doing a job properly. Besides, it was what he was paying for. The day before, he had secretly envied that tramp who bought his hunger for nothing, and had wondered . . . why not? . . . in future, just walk out? . . . with a sleeping-bag, perhaps?

Then he laughed and bit into the sausage roll. He bit into it for *her*. He owed it to her. She had chosen him for her confidence. Among the damp ferns and the moss and the stale pastry, they had grown that much closer. She had shown him her weakness, always a touching move on the part of a woman. Moreover there was something in all this event of secret vice, of forbidden fleshpots. And conspiracy again, the two of them together against the law, Slippery Joe himself! Besides, the sausage tasted damn good.

'You're a very wicked woman,' he said, eyeing her naughtily.

She tossed her head.

'You don't know the half of me yet,' she laughed. In the quiet green woodland shade her face-powder gleamed palely, her blue eyes shone from flattering shadows, and the thin touch of dark lipstick on her mouth, a fashion of other days, reminded him of the time of his young manhood. He almost said something about 'liking to know the other half of her', but it died on his lips.

'You know what?' he said instead, 'I feel twenty years younger.'

'It's the walnut sponge!' she laughed.

'No,' he said gravely, 'it's you.'

Together they stood for a few seconds in their dressing-gowns, in the wood, and stared at each other.

Then Mrs Mackay gave a little shiver, closed the tin, and murmured quietly that they ought to be getting back.

They walked away in silence. But close together. He could have said more, but that long look had already said as much as could now be borne. Later he thought. Very right of her to say we must go. Very right not to make things easy. It shows she's not . . . she's not . . . well, she's not.

But such a silence was not possible for very long: luckily a bird like a burglar in the bush startled a sudden 'Oh!' from her.

'Tigers!' he laughed, relieved. 'Lions!'

'Or our Keepers,' she smiled.

Across the lawn the great house rose up turret by turret to meet them, every window fired by the setting sun, a grotesque pile of yellow and purple with windows now of deadly bright tinsel. Framed by its screen of darkly billowing elms, it looked terribly sad, a lost vision of somebody else's childhood long ago. As they came to the lawn, the Colonel took Mrs Mackay's hand and pressed it.

'Good night,' he said quietly, 'it was lovely.'

Good night at six o'clock? It was usual down at the Hydro. Although many sat the evening out in the drawing-rooms of the big house, playing cards or watching television, most preferred the luxury of their beds. Colonel Hunt loved his, and hated the drawing-rooms. And gazebo dwellers of different sexes could hardly invite each other in, not with beds and wash-basins all around.

Set in his habits, it never even occurred to him that Mrs Mackay might like to sit up in the drawing-rooms. Even so, he would have avoided it. Enough for the day – he was no ardent young suitor. Besides, it was too public up at the house. Also, he was now nervous of how to proceed – and indeed of what the destination might be.

But he was moreover eager to taste one special pleasure of any young suitor – to sit alone somewhere and go over it all in his mind, to taste and taste it, experience it over again. He also wanted, more soberly, to assess what the hell was happening to him.

He telephoned for his apple and water, automatically looked through the television programmes, found there was a documentary on Dunkirk which happened to have been one of his first hard experiences as a thirty-year-old major, and got into bed. He switched the set on, and lay down. He thought of Deirdre Mackay, and idly watched the stukas dive.

In one way, these old flickerings of war might have occurred yesterday. But in another, they became mixed up with atmospheres of the 1914–18 War, which of course the Colonel had been too young to experience, but whose mood was now suggested by the presence of the great lawned garden outside, with its cedars and beeches and elms, a typical rest-home for the Flanders wounded: and time also had become muddled by the memory of Mrs Mackay's – of Deirdre's – face upturned in the woodland shade, of its thirty-ish make-up, and of his own abruptly young elation, somersaulting him back into the past, half in memory, half also as a strange new reality.

So, as now the guns boomed, and shook his toothbrush in a near-by glass, much of both past and present began to coincide – he closed his eyes and set himself to wonder about her: not about her life and husband, or even about her personality and character, but about her *thereness*, her actuality, a matter partly of physical appearance but mostly of those curious forces which isolate one person as overpoweringly unique, one among so many who might otherwise be thought fairly similar. There are other fish in the sea, to be sure: but which do you throw back, and why?

He knew this would lead him to thoughts of what, at a distance, can seem to be the most arbitrary of all attachments, love. Love, which feels so overwhelmingly unique, is on the way to being as repetitious as the next bull lumbering across the field to the waiting flanks of his cud-happy consort. Only the human brain, with its need to dignify itself, decorates and deifies an unavoidable animal process. Well, well – anyone knew that, so what's the use of going over it? But it set the blood racing: or rather, the mind most sweetly ringing.

Boom-boom went the guns. The great trees outside evoked ghosts of wounded officers and their flapper nurses. But the trees also brought him back to where he was, Elm Park. What effect was the place having on him? Might it not be as strong as a sea voyage, that well-known romancer? The same lifting of responsibility, a green kind of sea-change? Walking the gardens, close to the wide beauties of nature? The same throwing of passing people together ... and add the loss of weight, a perceptible lightness of mind materially proved by an occasional headache, and something else ... he searched for it ... yes, something not so romantic ... the intimate daily reminder that everyone here was largely a body, being daily pummelled about, everyone open to enemas and irrigation machines, everyone being opened up and all in it together. Matters normally private were tacitly out in the open.

The Colonel's mind was not one to speculate on any erotic

significances of the enema. But at the beginning of the week there had been a general lecture from Slippery Joe on the principles of his treatment. A lot had been said of such apparatus, and to a mixed audience: men and women sitting together in their dressing-gowns, faces like masks, had taken it without much flinching.

It had set a pace of some intimacy. No one would go so far as to say they were all one big family, nor did the staff say so. There was surprisingly little archness in the attitude of the staff. Someone indeed had labelled the huts 'gazebos', but mostly because once there had been an old gazebo thereabouts. And there was a habit of likening patients to their cars: 'Your engine's clogged and tired – isn't it just natural to come in for a decoking?' But this was, after all, perhaps the easiest way to get at the average contemporary mind. Though the allusion sometimes misfired, as indeed with Deirdre Mackay herself, who had been caught out with a petit beurre one morning. Without preamble, the nurse had said: 'Somebody's taking their car out of the garage too soon!'

'Wrong gazebo!' Mrs Mackay had said, swallowing her biscuit with relief. 'I have *no car*!' And had gone on to tell the astonished nurse at length, since she had spoken to no one yet that morning, what she thought of the impossibly selfish congestion of the roads today.

However, all in all the staff could be excused these attitudes. Enthusiasm is notably difficult to project, and turns easily to earnestness. Since the staff believed in their work, there was naturally sometimes a too sunny reverence of all things bright and natural.

Yes, the Colonel mused through the gunfire, this was very understandable – he himself had always found it difficult not to sound holy-boly when promoting certain health-some pursuits to troops who only wanted to drink themselves to death. And one had to agree that down here at the Hydro the air of eager belief proved finally effective, its very innocence lulled people back to secure and simple times lost somewhere in the past. In this, it was echoed by the building and gardens. Many of the middle-aged had by now retired to smaller homes in a tighter world. The herbaceous borders and smiling staff of Elm Park reminded them of easier days.

Altogether, on all these counts, it was a place of much potency.

The Colonel closed his eyes to the blue-flicking screen and thought, In for a penny, in for a pound, and tried again to conjure up Deirdre's face, the touch of her hand, and the extraordinary and almost immediate intimacy between them.

And this worried him. She had a husband, perhaps a reasonably contented life: and he himself had a sense of probity.

Accompanying such thoughts, the booming of the guns became ominous. And now they were abruptly interrupted by a voice from the night outside: 'Phyl! It's Dunkirk! *Phyl!*'

The call sounded tremendously close through the wooden summer house wall. It brought him back from real enough thoughts to reality itself. He looked at the back of his hand. Hairs and veins. *His* fingers. Him. God, he thought, what does one do next?

Deirdre Mackay in her gazebo thought about the Colonel. She was not watching television. She was up at the mirror watching herself. She was looking for something new in her face. And she found it, both in her mind's eye and in truth. 'I must look younger than I think,' her memory of the afternoon had told her: and indeed, excitement and interest had physically pulled her face together, certain droops were gone and she shone with affirmation.

She, too, was wondering at her behaviour. But unlike the Colonel she did not question outside influences, she was too used to things happening from inside. She had been through her Difficult Period. One or two years ago the strangest yearnings and irresponsibilities had possessed her. But this latest irresponsibility felt very different, it felt indeed responsible, and tender, and really rather beautiful. Yet she wondered: Am I going perhaps a bit soft? Have I really emerged from the menopause – is this part of another stage you have to go through?

Certainly her behaviour was unusual. She was not ordinarily flirtatious. She had always been faithful to Arthur. And Arthur was now sitting at home being faithful to her. Or rather, he would be at the club being faithful to her, guzzling a good meal, the pig. And here she was starving to death to lose a few pounds for him, which all appeared to be unnecessary: for did she not attract colonels like flies?

Colonels? No, just one tender and charming grey-moustached man, she thought more soberly, whom I like very, very much indeed. Who has somehow given me something I haven't felt for years: the sense of courtship, of being wanted, of being valuable.

Neither guilt nor any real question forced her thinking. The moment, rather than abstract possibility, was her concern. The affair was something immediately of the present, something to be felt again as soon as possible and to find out more about. Tomorrow, tomorrow . . .

Mrs Mackay, too, heard Hazel's night cry to Phyllis, but now only with pleasure. She smiled tenderly, remembering that similar cries from these two women had first brought Colonel Hunt to her.

Another windless, golden, October day. The Colonel felt fine. Night and its natural climate of doubts and fears had receded – all he too now wanted was to be by the side of his new friend as soon as possible.

But now, at nearly eleven o'clock, he still sat with his feet in cold water and his rump in a hot sitz bath. Opposite, clamped to a white-tiled wall, a clock with a big red hand jerked away the minutes until he should shift aside to a hot basin for his feet and a cold seat for his vitals.

The clock measured the minutes with a dreadful exactitude, demonstrating both the slow pace and the inexorable hunger of time. It symbolized all clocks. Nothing to do but sit – and the Colonel itched as impatient as a boy. It was a feeling he had not experienced for years.

A voice came from a cubicle next door to the sitz-bathroom. Somebody was having a colonic irrigation. 'This'll clear us right out, Mr Edie,' the voice said – it must have been the attendant's – 'and I want to hear those sixpences come tumbling out, yes, all the way back from last Christmas!'

The Colonel gave a great hoot of laughter. Really, this place, he thought, you'd never believe it – I must tell Deirdre! But of course, he could never tell Deirdre such a thing. Then again, he thought he could. Extraordinarily, yes, he could! You could trust yourself with her, she was so ... and he suddenly realized how he had never for a moment felt awkward with her. What a great boon this is! Trust, and all the small nervous fears dispensed with! I'm absolutely at ease with her, he thought.

His masseur's face came round the corner.

'Time's up! Why, you're *minutes* over!'

And so he was! Just thinking of her had destroyed time itself! Marvellous! He whipped a towel around him and began hurriedly to dry and dress. Lost time!

He found her out on the lawn reading the paper. 'Hello,' he said, 'no torture this morning?'

'Nothing today,' she smiled, taking off her glasses, 'and you?'

'Bongos and a sitz-bath. You wouldn't – you wouldn't mind if I bring up a chair?'

'I'd love you to,' she said easily. Then she pointed to where Mrs Davidson lay in her chaise-longue. 'But the best seats are taken. She's been there since dawn.'

He laughed, and fetched himself an ordinary deckchair.

For a long sunny while they sat together and talked. Everything, everything seemed interesting.

Along the paths and across those wide lawns the other

residents strolled. Isolated, they no longer looked in their dressing-gowns like the floral assembly of lunch-time. Against the soft green, or by beds of autumnal flowers, they passed like figures more devotional, both sexes gowned like monks habited in ethereal shades: occasionally female heads of grey hair, flat on top but curled closely round the back, had the appearance of tonsures.

Once or twice Colonel Hunt caught his companion glancing over towards Mrs Davidson stretched in the big chair.

'I don't know how she does it,' she murmured once.

'What?'

'Oh, nothing really.'

But when, at nearly one o'clock, Mrs Davidson rose, placed a ball of knitting and several magazines securely on the chair, and hurried off towards the laurel bushes where a little painted hand said 'toilets' Deirdre Mackay sighed: 'Oh, what a relief!'

'Eh?'

'She's been there, I swear, since eight o'clock. Holding on like grim death' and here she paused and gave him a glance of knowing modesty.

He understood, and laughed. Hers had been a simple enough remark; but his spirits rose right up, he went on chuckling – and then he did a dreadful thing, something not at all consonant with his real age. He leapt up, tipped Mrs Davidson's ball of knitting and magazines on to the lawn, and raced with the chair to the big beech, and propped it hidden behind.

He was already regretting it as he hurried back – wasn't he making an absolute ass of himself? – but thank God, found Mrs Mackay shaking with silent laughter. The act, silly as it was, sealed their conspiracy.

He only got back a second before Mrs Davidson came strolling, then stamping across the lawn to where her knitting lay.

'Well!' the single word rasped across the grass. *'Well!'*

Holding their breaths, they put their heads close together pretending to talk.

Mrs Davidson was already approaching and from several yards off called, 'Excuse me, but did you see anyone – ' but then broke off. For just at that moment, in horrible coincidence, two of the affluent North Country ladies came strolling across from nearby dahlia beds on their way back to the house.

Mrs Davidson was on to them in a trice.

'It's you!' she cried. 'You and your friends!'

The two ballooning pink peignoirs stopped. Two lacquered heads turned and glared. One spoke:

'I *beg* your pardon?'

'You've swiped my long-chair again!' shouted Mrs Davidson, quite lost in rage, 'I leave it for just two seconds and it's gone, it's *disgusting*, it's disgustingly *selfish*!'

The lacquered ladies smiled scornfully to each other, spreading their hands.

'Are *you* carrying a "long-chair", Isobel?' one said.

'Yes, darling, I've got about three tucked up in my bosom here.'

'It's your other friend then!' screamed Mrs Davidson. 'That's *my* ball of wool!' she yelled pointing, 'Thief!'

'But it wasn't your chair,' shouted back the woman called Isobel, coolness gone with the word thief. 'It's all our chairs!'

'It was my long-chair if my ball of wool was on it,' screamed Mrs Davidson.

The great balloon of peignoir advanced and now hissed back: 'Ball of wool! I'll ball-of-wool you! I've seen you hogging those chairs, I've seen you pinching them before anyone's had a sip of breakfast, *I've* seen you lying there hour after hour, hour after hour, like a great big toad. One of these days you'll burst your bladder, my good woman!'

The Colonel and Mrs Mackay looked at each other wildly. Aching, they stared out at the wooded horizon.

'Oh!' cried Mrs Davidson, 'You – you *common* woman!'

'Ooh-hoo! La-di-dah!'

Then another voice came belling across the lawn from the gazebos.

'I say, do you *mind*?' It was Hazel.

Mrs Davidson spun round and saw who it was. 'Coming from *you* . . .' she began.

Phyllis's head popped out. 'We can't hear our wirelesses!' she trilled, eyes wide with injured innocence.

The Colonel rose shakily. 'I can't bear it any longer,' he whispered.

They strolled off towards the beech, where he made Deirdre walk on a bit, pausing by the tree to call back politely:

'Excuse me – I couldn't help hearing something about a chair – there seems to be one behind here,' and walked on.

Mrs Davidson neither thanked nor suspected him. Her one thought was to get her long-chair. She left the others in mid-sentence and, as if in some desperate race, ran stumbling over to the tree. The last the Colonel and Mrs Mackay heard was a single victorious 'Ah!' from beneath the great russet dome of leaves.

'I say, I seem to have put the cat among the pigeons,' he said shamefacedly.

'Talk about bursting,' she laughed.

He shook his head: 'No, I shouldn't have done it.'

'You were sweet to let her have it back,' she said. And then: 'This *place*! Anything could happen here!'

'Yes. Anything,' he agreed, paused, and they looked at each other startled.

She lowered her eyes.

'Haze an' Phyl,' he said awkwardly, to cover the moment, 'like something you clean your teeth with.'

'Don't,' she said quietly, 'I don't want to laugh any more.'

He was touched. It had been a confession, a statement, and she had had the courage to make it. They strolled on in silence, aware again of something immense between them.

They returned to lunch, a single apple each. They parted for a rest in bed until tea-time. It was the ritual. Then at

31

half-past three tea – without milk or sugar – appeared, and this they took together outside the gazebos.

'A walk?' he said.

'Hungry?' she asked.

He shook his head. 'No,' he said. 'You must excuse me that. I really feel I should keep to the rules. After all, one's paying through the nose to be here,' he added to excuse himself. 'But I'll come along and watch.'

'No,' she smiled. 'You'll be my conscience, my strength.' And even this simple pleasantry brought him a kind of humble pride.

Not bothering to dress, they walked down the descending lawns in a direction away from the hollow oak, but again into woodland. Again the soft twilight of leaves overhead, the smells of moss and mouldering leaves. Bramble and bracken grew thick as walls to either side of the path. The silence drank in their footsteps soft on sand and leaves. The outside world seemed closed off, miles away. Almost immediately, only a dozen yards inside the wood they stopped, and listened to the silence, and turned to each other, and gently, chastely, kissed.

Somebody coughed.

The Colonel raised his head. Through a gap in the brambles, its colour doused in the green light, he saw the end of a garden chair, and Mrs Davidson's feet.

They hurried back out of the wood.

It was no use now. Eyes would be everywhere.

They laughed about it; but it was a brittle, anxious laugh. They walked on to where fields and farm buildings began, and stood looking at cows and pigs and hens. They leaned for a long time on a stile and watched the gentle rise and fall of fields and the darker wall of woods beyond.

The Colonel fretted. And a still darker absurdity riled him, a matter he never liked to face, that his own sexual powers had declined, that he might not be able to act if ... but there was scarcely that question? He had never actively thought of it ... and his troubled mind searched back at their momentary kiss and a further humiliation, this time in true clown's clothing, came to him. For, just these last two days, he had had a bad breath. He knew it, and he knew that this was why he had kissed so chastely, with closed lips. It was something to do with the starvation régime. So stringent a cleansing treatment brought out the very deepest poisons in the body; and so ironically even on water and fruit, each patient developed for a time this bad breath. And was this, he thought sadly, why she too had kissed so chastely, a modesty whose strange, girlish softness had touched him so?

'Damn!' he suddenly raged out aloud, spun round, and kissed her full and deep in the mouth.

'Oh,' she gasped at last, and shivered, and looked round. Only a cow watched them, slowly munching its cud.

'Don't worry,' he said, 'blast them all. All, all of them!'

But she shook her head, took his hand and led him away.

They walked hand in hand, with silences, with simple endearing lonely wonder – 'Dearest' – 'Darling' – until suddenly she stopped and faced him.

'Look,' she said, 'I've got to tell you. It's Sunday tomorrow and Arthur's coming down. I can't stop him, can I? I'm sorry – dearest, I *am* sorry.'

He nodded. There was not much he could say about it.

'If we went back,' she said quietly, 'to where other people are . . . just now . . . I think it would be easier.'

He kissed her softly again, and they walked back to the house.

That evening they did sit in the drawing-room, looking at magazines, idly talking – simply to be together.

Her husband had scarcely been spoken of before. She had mentioned him offhand once or twice, neither coldly nor with affection – more as an institution, an accoutrement. Of course, the Colonel had avoided the subject too, both in words and in his thoughts afterwards.

He was thus unprepared the next day for the shock of

seeing the two of them together. Yet there the man was, very much in the flesh and strolling by the dahlia beds he knew so well, a man dressed in tweeds and with Mrs Mackay walking beside him in her dressing-gown. Something unsavoury about that too, the tweeds and the night-clothes, something appallingly intimate.

The Colonel felt both jealous and guilty; he also felt a queer sympathy for this man who knew nothing of what had happened.

They seemed to have much to talk about as they strolled to and fro, they never stopped talking.

The Colonel sat a long way off, watching them covertly over his book. Mrs Davidson was back on the lawn – leaving them the woods out of kindness? Once, when their eyes met, she casually, perhaps kindly, looked away. The Colonel rose; this was too much, that old bitch being so nice. He would be better off inside his own gazebo. Among the chintzes and the cream walls and brown bakelite electric fittings, he sat and wondered where on earth it was all going to end.

The answer came later that afternoon, at five o'clock.

He happened to meet her on the path to the house, on a gravel path, with a high wall of dark laurel to one side, which he was to remember for a long time afterwards.

She was dressed. She had a hat on.

She came straight up to him and spoke clearly.

'I was looking for you. I was coming to find you,' she said. 'Arthur's asked me to go back to London with him. I'm going.'

He could not understand.

'Then – then I'll see you again – when, tomorrow?'

'I'm leaving,' she said, 'I'm not coming back.'

'Oh.'

'Dearest, I have to. Some, some things – I won't tell you what, they're personal and to do with the family – these things have happened. He can't deal with them alone. It's absurd, he even tried to persuade me to stay on. But I have to go. I can't let him down.'

'No.'

'It's to do with friends. A tragic happening . . .'

He searched all over her face, searching to get it, hold it for his memory. But he did say quietly, bitterly: 'And what's this?'

She lowered her head.

'I'm sorry.'

He tried to smile. 'It's rather sudden,' while a thousand voices shouted inside him, 'This is the moment! Seize it! Seize it!'

'I couldn't get away before. He helped me to pack. He's in the car now – waiting.'

She was gazing up at him, not going, waiting.

In the laurel's shade her white face and the huge moment hammered at him . . . whatever she had said, she stood now waiting for him to say or do something, the definitive thing . . . and the silence lengthened and at last it was she who moved, putting her face closer up towards him . . .

Abruptly he put out his hand and shook hers, and walked away, not trusting his voice to say even goodbye.

They never saw each other again. Colonel Hunt packed his bags and left the next day. It would have been impossible to continue with this sensible, outlandish treatment now.

Time, only time was left to heal what was never a great sorrow, but rather a sadness at having so bright a light suddenly lit, suddenly snatched away. He looked up her address, and several times nearly telephoned her. But he desisted. It would be underhand, it would mean lies, he was too old.

The years passed and it all became a memory; but he found that the light had not, after all, been quite taken away. In its own way, it shone on. It was a last romantic memory, a burst of light in the greying years. At his brasher moments, he even got rather bucked and proud of himself about it.

William Sansom

The Marmalade
Bird

Small brown birds the size of sparrows hopped about the breakfast verandah and occasionally said 'Tabib' to each other. Great crumb fanciers, it was after this piping little word that they were named.

'Tabib! Tabib!' Dr Livingstone squawked back at them from the indolence of silk pyjamas. 'Sod you Jack, I'm all right.'

'Speak for yourself,' his wife snapped.

'I'm speaking for the birds. It's what your little darlings are really saying. All birdsong is an aggressive vociferation of selfish possession. I've got a crumb, I've got a branch, I'm all right. You can hop it.'

'Rubbish,' she said. 'Yours is simply a nasty way of analysing what once was called the joy of life. A bird settles on a branch, likes it, and feels free to say how good everything is. Like you in the bathroom and "Old Man River".'

'Sod you Jill, the door's locked. As I said.'

'Then why the impassioned tremolo? Why the loving boom of those deep and ballsy base notes? You're having a good time and the whole hotel knows it.'

The doctor contained himself.

'Well,' he said after a while, unwisely not letting the subject drop, 'I suppose all joy of life has a selfish beginning.'

His wife gave him an irritating glance of triumph. 'As with anything else, there are degrees. There are degrees of

37

selfishness. Though I must say your own particular choice of song seems to cover them all.'

'Arguing with yourself again?'

'I'm simply saying these bass notes have a suspicious *me*-sound. But with you it could scarcely be otherwise.'

'No more than with your bloody tabibs.'

'Just because you're so mad about your marmalade bird.'

'You leave my marmalade bird alone. Beside, there's never been one sound from that poor bird's mouth.'

'Too full of marmalade.'

They were on holiday in Morocco. Morocco is a colourful place. It offers much that might be expected – white-robed riders blazing off muskets into a blue sky, a jet-black Royal Guard in vermilion uniforms, date-box sunsets, palms, veiled women and turbanned men.

But there is much also which we might not expect. Fields of rich Irish Atlantic green, with lonely camels standing about like humped banshees. Real Moorish rugs depicting stags at Scottish bay. Water-sellers dressed like Cambodian devils. And Blue Men in the south. Together with a variety of birds ranging from the ominous stork, clacking like a machine-gun from his look-out nest, to these minute tabibs and a certain long-beaked eccentric addicted, the Livingstones found, to marmalade.

The Livingstones had arrived in Marrakesh. Too late, of course, too hot already. 'But still,' they always consoled themselves, 'but still'. Anyway, they had many miles of pink mud town walls, orange trees spangling the pink with fruit like bright-balled Christmas trees, snake-swallowers in the market, swimming pools for the Europeans – it was idyllic, palmy and balmy, and with the High Atlas mountains showing a line of snow like white sherbet against near-Saharan heat.

'Hi, Atlas!' Dr Livingstone would genially greet these mountains each morning, while his wife silently gripped her tongue.

As with many another happily married couple, the

Livingstones spent part of each day marvelling at what they considered to be each other's unique selfishness. Blinded less by love than by propinquity, crippled by their very closeness, each magnified a few necessarily self-motivated gestures into mountains of egotism.

They picked on simple measures of self-survival or self-expression, without which no person claiming individuality could possibly exist, matters only really visible through the mutual idolization, almost the idolatry of a conjugal love jealous of pedestals, fearful of idols fallen.

For instance, Henry Livingstone was furious that Margaret insisted on this expensive hotel with its prices aimed at hard currency tourists – yet she was only after a bathroom and a balcony reassuring to her ordinary middle-class standards: and Margaret was livid with Henry for dragging her from the comforts of the hotel's tropical garden all the way to the central market square, there to stand by another and most inferior garden confected by a couple of itinerant hashish smokers. But Livingstone was showing no more than a normal masculine curiosity in his environment.

The hashish smokers, rolling-eyed men in rags, spent each evening putting on the dog for mixed crowds, black, brown, yellow, whitish, arrived from the surrounding country and from the desert to the south. They laid out a couple of long carpets, and placed on these two rows of old lemonade bottles sprouting with plastic leaves. Cheap jewellery was hung in the leaves to shine like flowers. Three tired-looking tame pigeons shuffled up and down this artificial paradise, greyly playing the peacock. At either end the two men smoked and chewed, occasionally shivering and shouting in ecstasy. To their drugged senses, the garden must have assumed a new and transcendental reality; much, thought Livingstone, as a window-box grows immense and lovely in the eyes of the gardenless Londoner exacerbated by vistas of brown brick.

But his wife pouted: 'When we've got ourselves a real

Garden of Paradise! And many a bird more than these middling pigeons! What about your marmalade bird? Isn't he preferable to you?'

Livingstone's eyes softened at the thought. But he replied smartly:

'This is a spiritual experience, an imaginary garden, far above the shrub of mere reality. A garden created by the brilliance of the mind – not a planted up thing like the hotel's. Why, there you just sit about being gardened at, it's as bad as television. Besides an orange could fall on your head. But these men go up to God for a few hours each night.'

'To rake in a handy few coppers down here on earth,' she said. 'I'm going home.'

'All right, Number One. I'll follow later.'

'Number One yourself.'

'And back to you, Mrs Tabib.'

'And to you. Tabib-bib-*bib*.'

So it went on. Always descending to a childish you-did, I-didn't, you-did. Back in the hotel he would silently sneer at her lotions and unguents laid out all over the best available table space, while he himself carelessly threw down his clothes on three separate chairs. When, on entering the room, she went instantly to the bathroom-lavatory, occupying this without question, he smiled secretly up at the chandelier. When she came out and found him sprawled in the best armchair, she muttered knowingly to all the other chairs.

Later, in bed, relaxed together or perhaps in the embrace of love, they forgot these small differences. They really got on quite well together. A happily married couple, you would say, of upper-middling means: enjoying for the most part the usual Marrakesh holiday round, visiting tombs and gardens, restaurants and markets, and sensibly living in the European quarter. Never trying to go native, as Livingstone rightly ruled: for then things would begin to look too reasonable. Keep it at eye's length, see it from the usual European view and maintain the illusion, the contrast.

The Livingstones, of course, were also usual in maintaining this mutual illusion of each other's selfishness. Only, at least once a day, the matter got out of control. This normally began somewhere towards the end of breakfast, when Margaret Livingstone's tabibs hopped all over the place, even flying into the room and settling on the bedstead or a jutting frieze ... and a discomfited Henry was left waiting, as always, for his marmalade bird which always arrived later – eyes on his wife's spoon in case it stole the bird's portion of marmalade.

The tabibs were small, industrious and brown. They came and went, dropping and rising like fat pellets of dung more than flying birds. Proles, he thought genially one morning. Not at all bad little fellows, but hardly in the same class as my long-beaked marmalader.

Then a pellet of prole whistled in past his ear, coming to rest inside the room on a painting of blue-faced berbers by a desert well. It was at least a chance to divert her from the marmalade.

'One of your tabibs has finished breakfast,' he muttered, 'and is inside squatting on the Art.'

'Cultured creature.'

'I said squatting. Hadn't you better – ?'

'Why, Henry, a little tabib? ... Good Lord, what's that?'

From below a sound of high-pitched whooping rose on the air. Livingstone flung down his paper and strode to the balcony wall, scattering tabibs right and left.

'*Will* you mind those birds, Henry!'

'It's those damned women again! They were at it yesterday. Picking all his oranges!'

'Ha! Now will you come back and let those tabibs break their fast in peace?'

'And ululating.'

'It's a beautiful sound. Traditional and feminine. Get your great male feet off those crumbs.'

'My heavens, they're up every single tree! This does look bad.'

Indeed, the row of orange trees in the street below was heavy with the bulging spotted dresses of berber women flinging down oranges into baskets beneath. As they worked, they kept up this strange bell-like bubbling of song. And down the oranges hailed in a storm of bright colour. A professional harvest. The trees would be picked clean.

'What's he going to do?' Livingstone muttered.

He was convinced that this odd bird could not be so roguish with the marmalade by chance, oranges must be his natural food.

'Don't you dare touch that marmalade,' he snapped – but immediately lowered his voice. 'Shh – he's here!'

And sure enough the exquisite fellow, head and shoulders above the others, with a fuselage spotted as a thrush and a beak like a little ibis, stood solemnly in the centre of the breakfast table and raised that sacred beak above the little marmalade jar.

And down the beak went, swift, vicious, exact. Livingstone held his wife's wrist, half to quieten her, half to make her share his own admiration. She felt his need – sighed and shared. Together they sat and watched the breakfasting bird. Up and down, head in the pot, head flicked up out and high, curved beak and long throat throttling down the sweetness. A fine, a Saracen beak, slender as the boom of a lateen sail ... an immaculate performance ... but still – *marmalade,* and there was something about the way he braced his legs busily apart before he dived his head in, something like a fat man bending at the wash bowl.

Margaret suddenly gave a high giggle.

The bird put its head to one side, scarcely liking to believe what it had heard, and then affronted flew off. Unaffected, the tabibs went on eating.

'Fool!' Dr Livingstone hissed. 'Can't you keep that bloody epiglottis quiet for one mortal second . . .'

'Ludicrous bird,' she laughed, opening her mouth wide.

He closed his and watched her. An unshared laugh looks

gluttonous. Selfish bitch, he thought. Thick-skinned selfish bitch.

Fury raged up. With anyone else, he would have disregarded so slight an episode. But with her it was part of a sum total, he lost all sensible control.

'Foof!' he shouted at the tabibs. 'Foo-oo-of!' And waved his arms.

The birds went on busily eating.

'You see?' he said excitedly 'Thick-skinned little morons! No wonder you like them, like to bloody like.'

Now she was laughing at him, he looked so absurdly angry. 'Oh Henry!' she snorted. He stood up and hurled a handful of travel brochures at the carefree birds. The brochures paused in mid-flight, opened like parachutes, and sank to the floor.

'Temper,' she laughed. 'My God, I wouldn't like to be one of your patients. Thank God – for once – we're married.'

He picked up a cushion and threw it hard in the middle of the birds, who now made off instantly. He turned and, thin-lipped, went off to the bathroom.

She followed him, furious.

'Great big bully,' she began, 'big, fat, redfaced, big, bully –'

He slammed the door in her face. On and on she went, gathering voice. He turned on all the taps loud. A little later his voice was heard again, in bravura, to make plain he was unaffected.

'Old Man River, it's Old Man River.'

She put her hands over her ears. 'My God,' she swore quietly at the big cool room, the hot African light burning up outside, 'My God.'

It was the beginning of a bad day but later, after a visit to the camel market, at luncheon, it was fairly patched up. They even laughed about it, trying to make it seem as ridiculous as it was. But there were undertones. At the market, she wanted to be photographed with a camel. He knew this was a racket for the camel-driver to get a tip, so he pretended the film was finished. She suspected it was not, but kept quiet, thinking: 'Mean old swine.' He knew she suspected him, and felt guiltily furious again. And when they returned to the hotel, she strode in straight in front of him – he missed the slight pause a woman should always give. And at lunch there occurred the most riling feature of all – she took all the butter on her plate in one selfish plunge of the knife. 'May one *perhaps* have some more butter?' he asked a passing waiter, loud and firm. The waiter pushed a second butter dish at him from behind a propped-up menu. He noticed her smile to herself. Found out, he dumbly fumed.

So it continued throughout the day. A quietly bubbling volcano: but with no open eruptions.

But that night, before going to bed, as she was lowering a metal shutter necessary as a shield against the dawn light, Margaret Livingstone saw, on a narrow ledge just where the heavy metal would come to rest, a mouse.

'Dr Livingstone!' she squeaked.

'Presume on,' he called from bed.

'There's a mouse under the shutter.'

'Squish.'

'Don't just lie there – come and help!'

He rose with a sigh from the bed. Always the same, just when he'd got settled. 'Get me a glass of water.' 'The curtain isn't quite drawn.' (Who'd got into bed first? she was thinking. Leaving her to shut the shutter?)

He went over and peered under the shutter. There indeed was the murky little creature huddled against the wall. A couple of feet of ledge to go: and a thirty foot drop. Nowhere to run to. But couldn't he frighten it a few inches along the ledge with his finger? Would it panic and throw itself over? *Mouse falls to its death*, he read. Yet if the shutter crashed down it would certainly be crushed ... and then one mouse-eye opened, a lizard-skinned eye, and gazed morosely up at him. He knew that look. It was no mouse at all.

'It's not a mouse, it's a – ' he called, and stopped himself just in time. Was the unspeakable little bundle wounded? It couldn't be as tame as all this?

'What is it?' Her voice from the bedroom, the voice which would say so very much more, all night long perhaps, if the bird was wounded.

But he knew, intuitively, his tabibs. The bird was simply roosting. It had chosen this place for the night, and nothing on earth, not even a dozen pounds of descending steel, was going to shift it.

She was there beside him, looking down.

'Yes,' he said, 'it's one of yours.'

'Oh the poor thing! Is it hurt? It must be hurt.'

'Roosting,' he whispered.

'How do you know?'

The bird was still looking gloomily up at them from one eye.

They watched for a minute as a light wind ruffled the small feathers. The bird huddled closer to the wall. 'Suppose it *is* hurt?' she asked.

'Then it's best left there. If it flew down, the cats'd get it. It's no good bringing it in, they usually die of shock.'

'Can't you feed it with your fountain pen?'

'You speak of the good old times. Ever tried to feed a bird with a biro? . . . look, I'll just shift it along an inch or two.'

'No!' she shrieked. The bird flicked its eye wide open, glared accusingly but never moved.

'Tabib or not tabib, that's the question,' he jovially tried. 'Darling, this shutter's *got* to be shut. It's the no-netting window, the mosquitoes – '

'Leave it open,' she said.

'We'll be bitten to death.'

'Come to think of it,' she said, 'I *have* got an old fountain pen – '

'Leave it open,' he said quickly.

'As *you* say. But do you think it's *all right*?'

'Like me to put the alarm on for three, getski upski and give it the kiss of life?'

'Don't be funny, you'd poison it.'

They turned back into the room, the shutter left a foot open. 'I'll never sleep,' she said, 'thinking of it.'

Ten minutes later he heard her regular soft snore.

But he lay awake.

Damn bird, damned woman. He listened into the dark. Soon enough, an angry little elastic band twanged high and the first mosquito came at him through the dark. 'Blast her!' he swore and struck himself in the face.

Silence again. Hit or miss? How deep the dark became when you stared into it! Dr Livingstone felt himself echoing into infinity. But the whine came again, desperate intimacy closed in – again he struck himself. How furious they sounded, hysterical with hunger. And he remembered them under the microscope, all barbed, sleek with wire hair, carrying a long scythe instead of a nose.

Silence again. The microscope brought back clinical memories – and the case of a sting that had proved fatal. So – for one tabib, one man? And what about malaria? Man versus tabib: you could multiply your tabibs on your hundred fingers – but could you do the same with your Henry Livingstones? He leapt from the bed, and tiptoed across the dark.

He found the window, and for a gross moment his hand reached forward to slam the shutter down on the roosting bird. But good sense stopped him. The Hippocratic oath, coupled with the furtive question 'How to dispose of the body?' sent his fingers instead raising the shutter to see more clearly. There indeed the bird still slept, while down in the lamplit street below a few cowled and veiled Moroccans passed from shadow to shadow. The scent of orange blossom rose thick and heady, a lightly laughing gas . . . as he reached down to tickle the bird's clasped wings. Surely it would just amble a few disgruntled steps sleepily forward?

A man in a djellaba passed into lamplight below – and from the corner of his eye Livingstone found the answer to a question which had been haunting him. All these past days such Arab figures had reminded him of something seen elsewhere before. And now at last he saw what it was. The djellaba was exactly the same, cut of hood and all, as a monk's robe. And the veiled women, with their dark long robes and the circular white blob at their faces, looked exactly like nuns. Precisely, in both cases, the medieval garment as preserved in the West. Now – had it been brought back from the crusades? Or was it just naturally the most practical and primitive workaday garment – no dispersion theory? He felt himself on the verge of the holiest of historical discoveries.

As his fingers reached forward: 'And I – St Francis of Assisi? Assisi – it's easy' – his mind sleepily muttered as the finger touched the bird, which flew swiftly off in the same moment.

He silently lowered the shutter, made his way across the dark to the bathroom to cover his face with deterrent – there would be quite a few of the brutes in the room by now – and found that she had taken the stuff to bed with her. Marvellous, wasn't it? As an alternative, he covered his face and neck with white antiseptic toothpaste and stumbled back to bed.

Anyway, the job was done. In the morning, it would be assumed the bird had taken to wing with the dawn.

But she woke up first and saw the shutter was closed.

It made a stormy beginning to the day, decorated by the medallions of several large mosquito bites on the doctor's browning skin. And worse; one of the bites had caught an upper eyelid, swelling it to a fat flaccid bag of flesh which now hung morosely down over half the eye, a fearful sight both to see and to see through, though not in itself dangerous. He looked like half a bloodhound.

'I tell you the bird *flew* off,' he swore.

'It would *look* like flying if it fell.'

And so on. Until her command to him to go downstairs and look for the corpse, and his flat refusal.

The breakfast tray came, and with it the morning's tabibs.

Feeding proceeded while the doctor tried not to scratch. He watched his wife's smile curve in pleasure upwards as she tossed crumbs here and there: it was like the curved smile of a cat, sweetly contented or selfishly cruel, as you wished. However, surrounded by the morning's birds, she appeared to be mollified. Nevertheless he kept, through his one good eye, as sharp a watch as he could on the marmalade pot.

Then, in the flurry of birds coming and going, rising and falling, and against the fine blue day beginning and the High Atlas shimmering its snow across the palm-tops, he suddenly saw a screwed-up wad of Kleenex fly from his wife's hand straight into the little hole of the marmalade pot top.

'By God!' he thundered. 'Holed in one!'

'What, darling?'

'Kleenex in the marmalade. *That's* what.'

'Oh piffle. We've finished long ago.'

'And with a starving bird shortly arriving?' he thundered. 'Don't you think of anything but your damned self?'

'Who killed cock robin – only last night?' she sweetly trilled back.

'I did *not* kill . . .'

'And bears the mark of Cain over his right eye?' she laughed savagely.

He rose to his feet with signs of formality. 'Your million tabibs have been fed. Would you mind now withdrawing from the table? My own single solitary bird's about due.'

In a spirit of armed frivolity, the Livingstones withdrew from the balcony to their room and sprawled back on long soft chairs to wait and watch.

The bird flew in immediately. It must have been sitting on one of its orange trees waiting for them to go. 'Clever Dick,' Margaret Livingstone murmured.

'Shh!'

There it stood again, the magnificent marmalade bird! Head and shoulders above the grovelling tabibs, peppered as a thrush, beaked as an ibis, and achieving even some of the important trousery strut of an eagle.

It went straight for the marmalade and with beautiful precision plunged its long beak into the pot.

Now the head would come up and the beak flute high in the air, swallowing the sweet juice in a silent, gobbling trill.

But the beak never came up.

It seemed to be stuck, the whole head seemed to be stuck in the pot.

The trousery little legs braced themselves and tugged. But the jar rose with the bird's head, just an inch or two off the tray, too light a jar to be pulled off, too heavy a jar to carry high. It was a bird in a glass mask which turned and faced Henry Livingstone. 'It's going for its little swim,' Margaret cooed, 'in its little goggles.'

Livingstone nearly struck her.

'Your damned Kleenex!' he swore. 'Now what are we going to do? I don't want to pull its head off.'

'No, darling,' she said.

'Well, for blood's sake *do* something!' he yelled.

'Me?'

'It's your fault!'

'It's your bird.'

'It's your responsibility!'

The bird was now backing away from itself in stumbling circles, knocking into cups, thrashing with its wings, bent and hump-backed as a miniature kiwi ... it staggered on to a piece of buttered toast, it thrashed up the sugar like a snow storm, once it raised the jar right up into the air, and stood like a feathered knight in a bright round helmet ...

Margaret whispered, 'You know ... but I don't like touching them ...'

Livingstone snorted.

'Sod you, Jack, I'm all right,' he muttered. 'Or rather, tabib to you.' And he tried to pick the bird up. It went mad, terrified, lurching everywhere at once. Livingstone snatched his hand away.

'God help us!' he simply said, and a tall Senegalese in baggy scarlet trousers and gold waistcoat entered the room carrying letters on a tray.

This man stood for a moment more astonished by humans than by bird: by the doctor's malevolent bloodhound eye and ghostly face patched with white toothpaste, by the wife with hair pinned mannishly down in a night-net. But his second thought, as servant and by nationality host to these strangers from the white North, was to be of assistance to the poor crazed things.

So that, as soon as the ghostly doctor had taken up the letters, he moved forward to edge the salver beneath the struggling bird, with a view to tossing it over the balcony to Kingdom Come.

Imperious in his giant colour and fine clothing, he stood for a second poised before racketing bird and pot into space as with a silver pingpong bat.

The doctor had assumed that, as with a white and black butler, this scarlet and black servant would now decorously withdraw with bird on tray in the traditional manner. But Margaret knew better. 'No!' she cried out, and at the same time reached forward both hands and delicately wrenched at bird and pot. She held her hands at arms' length and turned her face away, unable to watch her hand on the feathers, like a woman dealing with some kind of nauseous refuse.

The doctor humbly marvelled at this act of self-sacrifice.

The Senegalese stood astounded at her action, and suspicious that he himself was the reason for her averted face.

Margaret's left hand steadied the pot, which was all that had been needed all the time, and the bird was freed. It staggered for a second's dazed reorientation, its beak an ignoble fuzz of mashed Kleenex and marmalade rind. Lizard eyes half-closed, it had the cross-eyed look of a deep drinker.

And then, slowly because of the Kleenex, it opened its silent beak for the first and last time and enunciated in a broken voice well-known syllables never before heard so low and deferential:

'Taa-bib.'

It sounded, for the moment, like 'Thank you'.

Afterwards they agreed it must be one of those birds which imitated other cries for protective purposes. There on the silver tray held by the ramrod Senegalese, it was simply declaring that it was not there at all, that what they saw was no more than the next run-of-the-mill tabib.

But for the moment it sounded like a thank you, and more than that, a sudden and complete abnegation of all selfishness, a two-syllable essay in absolute humility.

It gathered itself together and took off. Shreds of Kleenex, falling like lonely white feathers, even like sighs, marked its flight.

'Thank you,' said Dr Livingstone to the Senegalese, who slightly inclined and withdrew on soundless slippers.

'Darling,' the doctor said to his wife, embracing her.

It was a moment when all their small differences, at least for the day, were solved. But of course, she could not resist it. *His* bird, *her* sacrifice, *his* exultation.

'Tabib?' she asked softly. 'Jacko?'

Jean Rhys

I Spy a Stranger

'The downright rudeness I had to put up with,' Mrs Hudson said, 'long before there was any cause for it. And the inquisitiveness! She hadn't been here a week before they started making remarks about her, poor Laura. And I had to consider Ricky, hadn't I? They said wasn't his job at the R.A.F. Station supposed to be so very hush-hush, and that he oughtn't to be allowed – '

While her sister talked Mrs Trant looked out of the window at the two rose beds in the front garden. They reassured her. They reminded her of last summer, of any day in any summer. They made her feel that all the frightening changes were not happening or, if they were happening, that they didn't really matter. The roses were small, flame-coloured, growing four or five on the same stalk, each with a bud ready to replace it. Every time an army lorry passed they shivered. They started shivering before you could see the lorry or even hear it, she noticed. But they were strong; hardened by the east coast wind, they looked as if they would last for ever. Against the blue sky they were a fierce, defiant colour, a dazzling colour. When she shut her eyes she could still see them as plainly as if they were photographed on her eyelids.

'They didn't stop at nasty remarks either,' said Mrs Hudson. 'Listen to this:

'People in this town are not such fools as you think and unless you get rid of that crazy old foreigner, that witch of Prague, who *you*

53

say is a relative, steps will be taken which you will not like. This is a friendly warning but a good many of us are keeping an eye on her and if you allow her to stay ...

This time next year ...

You'll be all very much the worse for wear.'

'That was the first,' she said. 'But afterwards – my dear, really! You think who, in a small place like this, who?'

'I might give a guess.'

'Ah, but that's the worst of it. Once start that and there's no end. It's surprising how few can be trusted. Here's a beauty. Written on quite expensive paper, too.'

' "A Gun for the Old Girls. . . ." A gun for the old girls?' Mrs Trant repeated. 'What's that mean?'

'There's a drawing on the other side.'

'*Well!*'

'Yes. When that came Ricky said "I can't have her any longer. You must tell her so." '

'But why on earth didn't you let me know what was going on? Malvern isn't the other end of the world. Why were you so vague?'

'Because it *was* vague. It was vague at first. And Ricky said "Take no notice of it. Keep quiet and it'll all blow over. And don't go and write a lot of gossip to anybody, because you never know what happens to letters these days. I could tell you a thing or two that would surprise you." So I said "What next? This is a free country, isn't it?" And he said there wasn't much free nowadays except a third-class ticket to Kingdom Come. And what could you have done about it? You couldn't have had her to stay. Why, Tom detests her. No. I thought the best thing was to advise her to go back to London.'

And hadn't she tried to be as nice as possible and to speak as kindly as she could?

'Laura,' she had said, 'I hate to tell you, but Ricky and I think it best that you should leave here, because there's such a lot of chatter going on and it really isn't fair on him. The blitz is over now, and there are all these divan rooms that are advertised round Holland Park or the Finchley Road way. You could be quite comfortable. And you can often find such good little restaurants close by. Don't you remember the one we went to? The food was wonderful. The one where the menu was in English on on side and Continental on the other?'

'What do you mean by Continental?'

'Well, I mean Continental – German, if you like.'

'Of course you mean German. This Anglo-German love-hate affair!' she had said. 'You might call it the most sinister love affair of all time, and you wouldn't be far wrong . . .!'

'She could be very irritating,' Mrs Hudson continued. 'She went on about London. "I daresay, Laura," I said, "I daresay. But London's a big place and, whatever its disadvantages, it has one advantage – there are lots of people. Anybody odd isn't so conspicuous, especially nowadays. And if you don't like the idea of London, why not try Norwich or Colchester or Ipswich? But I shouldn't stay on here." She asked me why. "Why?" I said – I was a bit vexed with her pretending as much as all that, she must have known – "Because somebody has started a lot of nasty talk. They've found out that you lived abroad a long time and that when you had to leave – Central Europe, you went to France. They say you only came home when you were forced to, and they're suspicious. Considering everything, you can't blame them, can you?" "No," she said, "it's one of the horrible games they're allowed to play to take their minds off the real horror." That's the sort of thing she used to come out with. I told her straight, "I'm sorry, but it's no use thinking you can ignore public opinion, because you can't." "Do you wish me to leave at once?" she said, "or can I have a few days to pack?" Her face had gone so thin. My dear, it's dreadful to see somebody's face go thin while you're watching. Of course, I assured her she could have all the time she wanted to pack. If it hadn't been for Ricky I'd never have asked her to go, in spite of that hound Fluting.'

'Oh Lord,' said Mrs Trant, 'was Fluting mixed up in it?'

'Was he? Was he not? But it was her own fault. She got people against her. She behaved so unwisely. That quarrel with Fluting need never have happened. You see, my dear, he was dining here and he said some of the Waafs up at the Station smelt. And he was sarcastic about their laundry allowance. "Pah!" he said. Just like that – "Pah!" *Most* uncalled for, I thought, especially from a man in his position. However, what can you do? Smile and change the subject – that's all you can do. But she flew at him. She said, "Sir, they smell; you stink." He couldn't believe his ears. 'I *beg* your pardon?" – you know that voice of his. She said "Inverted commas". He gave her *such* a look. I thought "You've made an enemy, my girl".'

'I call that very tactless – and badly behaved too.'

'Yes, but tactless and badly behaved on both sides, you must admit. I told her "It's better not to answer them. Believe me, it's a mistake." But she thought she knew better. It was one silly thing like that after another, making enemies all over the place. ... And she brooded, she worried,' said Mrs Hudson. 'She worried so dreadfully about the war.'

'Who doesn't?'

'Yes, but this was different. You'd have thought she was personally responsible for the whole thing. She had all sorts of cracky ideas about why it started and what it meant.'

'Trying to empty the sea with a tin cup,' Mrs Trant said sadly.

'Yes, just like that. "It's too complicated," I said to her one day when she was holding forth, "for you to talk about the why and the wherefore." But she had these cracky ideas, or they'd been put into her head, and she wanted to try to prove them. That's why she started this book. There was no harm in it; I'm sure there was no real harm in it.'

'This is the first I've heard about a book,' said Mrs Trant. 'What book?'

Mrs Hudson sighed. 'It's so difficult to explain. ... You remember all those letters she used to write, trying to find out what had happened to her friends? Through the Red

Cross and Cook's and via Lisbon, and goodness knows what?'

'After all, it was very natural.'

'Oh yes. But suddenly she stopped. She never had any news. I used to wonder how she could go on, week after week and month after month, poor Laura. But it was curious how *suddenly* she gave up hope. It was then that she changed. She got this odd expression and she got very silent. And when Ricky tried to laugh her out of it she wouldn't answer him. One day when he made a joke about the Gestapo getting her sweetheart she went so white I thought she'd faint. Then she took to staying in her room for hours on end and he didn't like it. "The old girl's got no sense of humour at all, has she?" he said. "And she's not very sociable. What on earth does she do with herself?" "She's probably reading," I said. Because she used to take in lots of papers – dailies and weeklies and so on – and she *hung* about the bookshops and the library, and twice she sent up to London for books. "She was always the brainy one of her family." "Brainy?" he said. "That's one word for it." I used to get so annoyed with him. After all, she paid for the room and board and the gas meter's a shilling in the slot. I didn't see that it was anybody's business if she wanted to stay up there. "If you dislike her so much, it's all to the good, isn't it?" I said. But that was the funny thing – he disliked her, but he couldn't let her alone. "Why doesn't she do this, and why doesn't she do that?" And I'd tell him "Give her time, Ricky. She's more unhappy than she lets on. After all, she'd made a life for herself and it wasn't her fault it went to pieces. Give her a chance." But he'd got his knife into her. "Why should she plant herself on us? Are you the only cousin she's got? And if she's seen fit to plant herself on us, why can't she behave like other people?" I told him she hadn't planted herself on us – I invited her. But I thought I'd better drop a hint that was the way he felt. And there she was, my dear, surrounded by a lot of papers, cutting paragraphs out and pasting them into an exercise-book. I asked what she was doing and if I could have a look. "Oh, I don't think it will interest you," she said. Of course, that was the thing that, when the row came, they had most against her. Here it is – the police brought it back. Ricky said I must destroy it, but I wanted to show it to you first.'

Mrs Trant thought 'First those horrible anonymous letters, now a ridiculous exercise-book!' She said, 'I don't understand all this.'

'It's what I told you – headlines and articles and advertisements and reports of cases in court and jokes. There are a lot of jokes. Look.'

The exercise-book began with what seemed to be a collection of newspaper cuttings, but the last pages were in Laura's handwriting, clear enough at first, gradually becoming more erratic, the lines slanting upwards, downwards, the letters too large or too small.

'It was only to pass the time away,' Mrs Hudson said. 'There was no harm in it.'

'No, I suppose not.'

Mrs Trant turned to the handwriting at the end.

She said, 'The top part of this page has been torn out. Who did that?'

'I don't know. The police, perhaps. It seems they had a good laugh when they read it. That must have been one of the funniest bits.'

Mrs Trant said 'A forlorn hope? What forlorn hope?'

'. . . a forlorn hope. First impressions – and second?

An unforgiving sky. A mechanical quality about everything and everybody which I found frightening. When I bought a ticket for the Tube, got on to a bus, went into a shop, I felt like a cog in a machine in contact with others, not like one human being associating with other human beings. The feeling that I had been drawn into a mechanism which intended to destroy me became an obsession.

I was convinced that coming back to England was the worst thing I could have done, that almost anything else would have been preferable. I was sure that some evil fate was in store for me and longed violently to escape. But I was as powerless as a useless, worn-out or badly-fitting cog. I told myself that if I left London I should get rid of this obsession – it was much more horrible than it sounds – so I wrote to the only person whose address I still had, my cousin Marion Hudson, hoping that she would be able to tell me of some place in the country where I could stay for a while. She answered offering me a room in her house. This was at the end of what they called the "phoney war" ...'

'But she seems to be writing to somebody,' said Mrs Trant. 'Who?'

'I've no idea. She didn't tell me much about herself.' Mrs Hudson added, 'I was pleased to have her. She paid well and she was good about helping me in the house, too. Yes, I was quite pleased to have her – at first.'

'... the "phoney war", which was not to last much longer. After I realized I was not going to get answers to my letters the nightmare finally settled on me. I was too miserable to bear the comments on what had happened in Europe – they were like slaps in the face.

I could not stop myself from answering back, saying that there was another side to the eternal question of who let down who, and when. This always ended in a quarrel, if you can call trying to knock a wall down by throwing yourself against it, a quarrel. I knew I was being unwise, so I tried to protect myself by silence, by avoiding everybody as much as possible. I read a great deal, took long walks, did all the things you do when you are shamming dead.

You know how you can be haunted by words, phrases, whole conversations sometimes? Well, I began to be haunted by those endless, futile arguments we used to have when we all knew the worst was coming to the worst. The world dominated by Nordics, German version – what a catastrophe. But if it were dominated by Anglo-Saxons, wouldn't that be a catastrophe too? Then, of course, England and the English. Here everybody, especially Blanca, would become acrimonious. "Their extraordinary attitude to women." "They're all mad." "That's why." And so on. Blanca's voice, her face, the things she used to say haunted me. When I had finished a book I would imagine her sharp criticisms. "What do you think of that? Isn't it unbelievable? What did I tell you? Who was right?" All these things I could hear her saying.

And I began to feel that she wasn't so far wrong. There is something strange about the attitude to women as women. Not the dislike (or fear). That isn't strange of course. But it's all so completely taken for granted, and surely that is strange. It has settled down and become an atmosphere, or, if you like, a climate, and no one questions it, least of all the women themselves. There is *no* opposition. The effects are criticized, for some of the effects are hardly advertisements for the system, the cause is seldom mentioned, and then very gingerly. The few mild ambiguous protests usually come from men. Most of the women seem to be carefully trained to revenge any unhappiness they feel on each other, or on children – or on any individual man who happens to be at a disadvantage. In dealing with men as a whole, a streak of subservience, of servility, usually appears, something cold, calculating, lacking in imagination.

But no one can go against the spirit of a country with impunity, and propaganda from the cradle to the grave can do a lot.

I amused myself by making a collection of this propaganda, sometimes it is obvious, sometimes sly and oblique, but it's constant, it goes on all the time. "For Blanca." This is one way they do it, not the most subtle or powerful way of course.

Titles of books to be written ten years hence, or twenty, or forty, or a hundred: *Woman an Obstacle to the Insect Civilization? The Standardization of Woman, The Mechanization of Woman, Misogyny –* well, call it misogyny – *Misogyny and British Humour* will write itself. (But why pick on England, Blanca? It's no worse than some of the others.) *Misogyny and War, The Misery of Woman and the Evil in Men or the Great Revenge that Makes all other Revenges Look Silly.* My titles go all the way from the sublime to the ridiculous.

I could have made my collection as long as I liked; there is any amount of material. But why take the trouble? It's only throwing myself against the wall again. You will never read this, I shall not escape.'

Mrs Trant, who had been frowning at the words *Misogyny and War*, exclaimed indignantly 'Couldn't she find something else to occupy her mind – now, of all times?'

'Do you know,' said Mrs Hudson, 'there are moments – don't laugh – when I see what she meant? All very exaggerated, of course.'

'Nonsense,' Mrs Trant repeated, examining sketches of narrow, sharp-nosed faces in the margins of the last few pages.

'I am very unpopular in this damned town – they leave me in no doubt about that. A fantastic story about me has gone the rounds and they have swallowed every word of it. They will believe anything, except the truth.

'Sometimes people loiter in the street and gape up at this house. The plane tree outside my window has been lopped and they can look straight into my room, or I think they can. So I keep the curtains drawn and usually read and write in a very bad light. I suppose this accounts for my fits of giddiness.

'Why do people so expert in mental torture pretend blandly that it doesn't exist? Some of their glib explanations and excuses are very familiar. I often think there are many parallels to be drawn between – '

Here the sentence broke off. Mrs Trant shook her head and shut the exercise-book. 'What a stifling afternoon!' she said. 'Too much light, don't you think?'

She glanced at the roses again and decided that their colour was trying. The brilliant, cloudless sky did that. It made them unfamiliar, therefore menacing, therefore, of course, unreal.

'It's all very well to say that nobody liked Laura,' she thought. 'Judy liked her.'

Judy was her youngest daughter and the prettiest. But too moody, too fanciful and self-willed. She had stood up to her father about Laura. It had been amusing at the time, but now she wasn't so sure – a girl ought to play safe, ought to go with the tide, it was a bad sign when a girl liked unpopular people. She imagined Judy growing up to be unhappy and felt weak at the knees, then suddenly angry.

She must have said 'Judy' aloud, because Mrs Hudson remarked 'You worry too much about Judy. She's all right – she's tough.'

'She's *not* tough,' thought Mrs Trant. 'She's the very reverse of tough, you sterile old fool.'

She moved her chair so that she could not see the rose beds and said 'Well, if you told Ricky about these hallucinations, I don't wonder there was a row.'

'I never told him.'

'Well, why was there all this trouble? Did she seem crazy? Did she look crazy?'

'No, not exactly. Only a very strained expression. I don't know why they made such a dead-set at her. Her *gift* for making enemies, I suppose.'

'Fluting?'

'Not only Fluting. She was so careless.'

– Careless! Leaving the wretched book lying about, and that daily woman I had spread a rumour that she was trying to pass information on to the enemy. She got on the wrong side of everybody – everybody –

'You know old Mr Roberts next door – well, she quarrelled with him. You can't imagine why. Because his dog is called Brontë, and he kicks it – well, pretends to kick it. "Here's Emily Brontë or my pet aversion," he says, and then he pretends to kick it. It's only a joke. But Ricky's right; she has no sense of humour. One day they had a shouting match over the fence. "Really, Laura," I told her, "You're making a fool of yourself. What have you got against *him*? He's a dear old man." She gave me such a strange look. "I don't know how you can breathe after a lifetime of this," she said . . .

'Well, things did go very wrong, and after the anonymous letters came, Ricky said I must get rid of her. "When is she going?" he would say, and I would tell him "One day next week." But the next week came and she didn't go, and the week after that, and she didn't go . . .'

– I should have insisted on her leaving, I see that now. But somehow I couldn't. And it wasn't the three guineas a week she paid. I said two, but she said it wasn't enough. Three she gave me, and goodness knows it's nice to have a little money in your pocket without asking for it. Mind you, I wouldn't say that Ricky is a mean man, but he likes you to ask; and at my age I oughtn't to have to ask for every shilling I spend, I do think. But it wasn't that. It went right against the grain to turn her out when she was looking so ill. Seven stone ten she weighed when she left. Even the assistant in the chemist's shop looked surprised.

Then the day when I was going to give her another hint, she said 'I've started packing'. And all her things were piled on the floor. Such a lot of junk to travel about the world with – books and photographs and old dresses, scarves and all that, and reels of coloured cotton.

A cork with a face drawn on it, a postcard of the Miraculous Virgin in the church of St Julien-le-Pauvre, a china inkstand patterned with violets, a quill pen never used, a ginger jar, a box full of old letters, a fox fur with the lining gone, silk scarves each with a history – the red, the blue, the brown, the purple – the green box I call my jewel case, a small gold key that fits the case (I'm going to lock my heart and throw away the key), the bracelet bought in Florence because it looked like a stained glass window, the ring he gave me, the old flowered workbox with coloured reels of cotton and silk and my really sharp scissors, the leather cigarette case with a photograph inside it. . . . Last of all, the blue envelope on which he wrote 'Listen, listen', in red chalk . . .

'When I told Ricky "She's going, she's packing her things," he said "Thank God. That's the best news I've heard for a long while." But it was the next night that it happened. We were down in the kitchen. The worst raid we've had – and no Laura. I said "Do you think she's asleep?" "How could anybody sleep through this? She'll come when she's ready. I expect the zip in her ruddy siren suit's got stuck," Ricky said, and I had to laugh. . . . You know, he really was horrid to her. "What's the old girl want to clutter up the bathroom for?" he'd say, and I'd say "Well be fair, Ricky, she must wash, whatever her age is. If she didn't it would only be another grievance against her. . . . She had some good clothes when she first came and she used to make the best of herself. "These refugees!" he'd say, "all dressed up and nowhere to go." Then she got that she didn't seem to care a damn what she looked like and he grumbled about that. She aged a lot too. "Ricky," I said, "if you do your best to get people down you can't blame them when they look down, can you?" Sometimes I wonder if she wasn't a bit right – if there isn't a very nasty spirit about.'

'But there always has been,' Mrs Trant said.

'Yes, but it's worse now, much worse. . . . Well, when the lull came I rushed upstairs. She was smoking and playing the gramophone she'd bought, and as I came in the record stopped and she started it again. "Laura," I said, "*is* this the moment to fool about with *music*? And your black-out's awful." While I was fixing it I heard the warden banging at the door and shouting that we were showing lights. "I thought so," she said. "The Universal Robots have arrived," and something about *R.U.R.* Then she went to the head of the stairs and called out to the warden "The law? The law! What about the prophets? Why do you always forget them?" In the midst of this the All Clear went. Ricky said to me "That's enough now. She's as mad as a hatter and I won't stand for it a day longer. She *must* get out." I decided not to go to bed at all, but to do my shopping early for once, and as soon as I was in the butcher's I knew it had got round already – I knew it by the way people looked at me. One woman – I couldn't see who – said "That horrible creature ought to be shot." And somebody else said "Yes, and the ones who back her up ought to be shot too; it's a shame. Shooting's too good for them." I didn't give them any satisfaction, I can tell you. I stood there with my head up, as if I hadn't heard a word. But when I got back here the police were in the house. They'd been waiting for a pretext – not a doubt of that. They said it was about the lights, but they had a warrant and they searched her room. They took the book and all her letters. And at lunch-time Fluting telephoned to Ricky and said there was so much strong feeling in the town that something must be done to get her away at once. ... I don't know how I kept so calm. But I look older too, don't you think? Do you wonder? ... After the police left she went upstairs and locked herself into her room and there she stayed. I knocked and called, but not a sound from her. When Fluting telephoned Ricky wanted to break the door down. I've never seen him in such a state – my dear, green with rage. I said No, we'd get Dr Pratt, he'd know what to do.'

'And did Dr Pratt say she was insane? What a terrible thing!'

'No, he didn't, not exactly. She opened the door to him at once and when he came downstairs Ricky talked about getting her certified. "I'll do nothing of the sort," Pratt said. "There's too much of that going on and I don't like it." '

'Pratt's an old-fashioned man, isn't he?'

'Yes, and obstinate as the devil. Try to rush him and he'll go bang the other way. And I got a strong impression that somebody else has been on at him – Fluting, probably. "She's been treated badly," he said, "from all I can hear." "Well," Ricky said, "why can't she go somewhere where she'll be treated better? I don't want her here." Pratt said he knew that the police weren't going to press any charge. "They hadn't any charge to press," I said, "except the light – and goodness knows it was the *merest glimmer*." And he smiled at me. But he told us it was advisable for Laura to leave the town. Wasn't there any friend she could go and stay with, because it would be better for her not to be alone? We said we didn't think there was – I remembered what you told me about Tom – and we all went up to her room. Pratt asked her if she was willing to go to a sanatorium for a rest and she said "Why not?" Ricky shouted at her "You get off to your sanatorium pronto. You ought to have been there long ago." "You're being inhuman," Pratt said. Ricky said "Well, will the bloody old fool keep quiet?" Pratt told him he'd guarantee that.'

'Inhuman,' said Mrs Trant. 'That's the word that keeps

coming into my head all the time now – inhuman, inhuman.'

Her sister went on 'And she was perfectly all right until the last moment. The taxi was waiting and she didn't come down, so I thought we'd better go and fetch her. "Come along, old girl," Ricky said. "It's moving day." He put his hand on her arm and gave her a tug. That was a mistake – he shouldn't have done that. It was when he touched her that she started to scream at the top of her voice. And swear – oh my dear, it was awful. He got nasty, too. He dragged her along and she clung to the banisters and shrieked and cursed. He hit her, and kicked her, and she kept on cursing – oh, I've *never* heard such curses. And I wanted to say "Don't you dare behave like that, either of you," but instead I found I was laughing. And when I looked at his face and her face and heard myself laughing I thought "Something has gone terribly wrong. I believe we're all possessed by the Devil. . . ." As soon as we got into the garden Ricky let go of her, a bit ashamed of himself, I will say. She stood quietly, looking around, and then – d'you know what? – she started talking about the roses and in quite a natural voice "How exquisite they are!" "Aren't they?" I said, though I was shaking all over. "They weren't here," she said, "last time I went for a walk." I said "They come out so quickly, so unexpectedly. Have one for your buttonhole." "No, let them live," she said. "One forgets the roses – always a mistake." She stood there staring at them as if she had never seen roses before and talking away – something about how they couldn't do it, that it wouldn't happen. "Not while there are roses," she said two or three times. Quite crazy, you see, poor Laura, whatever Pratt's opinion was. "The taxi's waiting, dear," I said, and she got in without any fuss at all.'

'Is this the place?' Mrs Trant said.

There was a photograph on the cover of a prospectus showing a large, ugly house with small windows, those on the two top floors barred. The grounds were as forbidding as the house and surrounded by a high wall.

'I don't like this place.'

'What was I to do, my dear? The sanatorium Pratt suggested was far too expensive. She's got hardly any money left, you know. I had no idea how little she had. What will happen when it's all gone I daren't think. Then Ricky got on to this place near Newcastle. I showed her the prospectus. I asked her if she minded going and she said "No". "You do realize you need a rest, don't you?" I said. "Yes," she said, "I realize that." She can come away if she wants to.'

'Can she, do you think?'

'Well, I suppose she can. I must say the doctor there doesn't seem – I know I ought to go and see her, but I dread it so. I keep on putting it off. Of course, there's a golf links there. Not much of a garden, but a golf links. They can play golf as soon as they're getting better.'

'But does she play golf?' said Mrs Trant.

'Let's hope,' said Mrs Hudson, 'let's hope ...'

Jean Rhys

Temps Perdi

'Rolvenden' is a square, red-brick house, and it stands with two others on the farthest outskirts of a good-sized village on the east coast. It belongs to one of the masters of a small public school which has moved to Gloucestershire for safety's sake. There is nothing in the house that you can say is ugly; on the other hand there is nothing that you can say is beautiful, impulsive, impetuous or generous. All is sparse, subdued, quiet and negative, or so you would think – a lawn, a large vegetable garden, an empty garage and, when I first came, a few last sad flowers. Outside the front door a gravel path, once bordered with lavender, leads to a green gate.

The two other houses have been taken over by the Army. The one opposite has large grounds and I never hear a sound from it. But from the one on the side there is often the clatter of men washing up ill-temperedly. How they chuck the things about! This is the time of smash and grab. Some poor devil – or rich devil or stupid devil – had tried hard with that house. There are four bathrooms – pink, black, green and blue. But there is venom in the way those men wash up, and there won't be much left of the pink, black, green and blue bathrooms when the military have got out.

But why be glad? Above all, why be sad? Death brings its own anaesthetic, or so they say . . .

Behind the garden wall there is land and a row of cottages. Never a sound from them either. At first I thought there wasn't a living soul there, but I learnt better later.

In justice to 'Rolvenden' I must say that it has changed a great deal since I have lived in it, and in fairness to myself I must add that I knew at once that we shouldn't get on and argued that I did not want to live there alone – especially in October, November, December and January. But there are times when one is helpless. However, only the helpless know this – and why preach to the converted?

A few days ago, or a week ago – I have forgotten – it began to snow. Since then I have been quite happy. Yes, since the snow started falling I have been much happier, though I don't trouble to look at it. Why look at it when I remember so well the first time I saw it? It was better then – it was a marvel, the only thing in England that hadn't disappointed me. (Remembering when I used to have to touch and taste it every time it fell . . .)

Now, on my way to the garage in the morning to bring in coal, I see the black trunks of the trees in the garden and the thin, pointing branches, then hurry in to light the fire and make my bacon sandwich and cup of coffee essence. After that I can lie for a long time watching the neutral sitting-room and the rows of extraordinary books without being angry or afraid or hoping. Now I am almost as wary of books as I am of people. They also are capable of hurting you, pushing you into the limbo of the forgotten. They can tell lies – and vulgar, trivial lies – and when there are so many all saying the same thing they can shout you down and make you doubt, not only your memory, but your senses. However, I have discovered one or two of the opposition. Listen: '. . . to conduct the transposition of the souls of the dead to the White Island, in the manner just described. The White Island is occasionally also called Brea, or Britannia. Does this perhaps refer to White Albion, to the chalky cliffs of the English coast? It would be a very humorous idea if England was designated as the land of the dead . . . as hell. In such a form, in truth, England has appeared to many a stranger.' (To many a stranger . . .)

Also I have discovered how to keep warm. You drape a blanket over the door, which stops the draught from the keyhole and the cracks, and a bolster finishes it off. And now I know how to pile the cushions so that I can sit on the floor in front of the fire without slipping backwards. The solid, uncomfortable chairs help. I am learning how to make use of you, my enemy.

The piano is out of tune. It gives a cracked, shattered and ghostly sound, it complains like a hurt animal when I play 'Mama, I want to make rhythm, I want to make music' and 'Time on my hands', then backwards to 'Si j'avais su – évidemment', backwards again to the waltz of Nina Rodriguez, never forgotten, heard so long ago.

Said to be twelve, Nina was probably sixteen or seventeen. She was a performer in a Havana circus which was touring the smaller Caribbean islands. It was the first theatrical performance I had ever seen. The circus tent was as huge as a cathedral to me, and the trapeze impossibly high and frail. It was lighted by glaring acetylene lamps.

The Rodriguez family were the stars. Mr Rodriguez, burly and sinister, always wore light-blue tights; Madame Rodriguez, pale, sad and mournful under her make-up, wore pink or red, and lovely Nina – the Only Girl Who Works Without a Net – wore black. Black tights to match her black eyes. And her golden curls were hanging down her back, too. We craned our necks to watch her, a black and gold butterfly caught in a web, weaving in and out of the web, miraculously escaping, miraculously coming to earth again, giving the two little stylized hops, smiling, kissing her hands to us.

Pale Madame Rodriguez worked on a higher trapeze. The net was brought in with much ceremony and there was a big roll of drums for the dangerous bit, but it wasn't the same thing and I don't remember a note of her waltz.

I was in the kitchen making a bacon sandwich when the coal arrived. It had been worrying me – there was so little left in the garage and all the coal in the bin outside the kitchen had disappeared. The people from the cottages in the lane took most of it – at first surreptitiously when I was out; after they had sized me up, openly.

The clatter of coal on zinc. Then a man's voice said, 'That's the bathroom.'

'Well what about it? Why are you looking at it? Is there a woman in the ditch?' said a second voice.

'Why d'you think I'd look at her if there was?' the first voice said, very offended. 'Why should you think I'd look at a blank, blank cow in a blank, blank, blank ditch?'

I walked out of the kitchen and scowled at them. These people are altogether too much. . . . They jeered back at me.

'You shouldn't have put the coal in that bin,' I said in an old shrew's voice. 'You should have asked me. You should have put it in the garage. Every lump of it will get stolen there. It was full when I came and it's all gone now because there are a lot of thieves round here, and mean thieves too. There are meaner thieves here than anywhere I've ever been in my life.'

'A-ah?' said the one of them.

'It ought to have a padlock on it,' the second one said, helpfully. 'What can you expect if it hasn't got a padlock on it?'

They both wear the local mask – beige in colour as usual.

'Go to hell,' I said.

The first man answered gently, 'Yes, it's very cold today, isn't it, Miss?'

The second one said, 'Very cold weather. Madam,' he said, winking at the first one.

They went off and I started after them. They must be frozen. Shall I call to them and ask them in to have some coffee essence? They might warm the place.

But before they got to the garden gate – 'Rolvenden' is painted on it – I saw that they were shaking with laughter.

Silent, smothered laughter – never, even with them, a good, hearty shout or curse, just this silent, sly, shy laughter. I can imagine what they would have said about me if I had asked them indoors.

That's an exaggeration. They don't think or say anything that I would imagine they would think or say. Speak for yourself and no falsities. There are enough falsities; enough harm has been done.

For all that was left of the afternoon I carried scuttles of coal from the bin outside the kitchen to the garage, which can be locked, and the house watched me haughtily, seeing me as I really am. And once or twice I looked back at it and thought that maybe I too saw it as it really was. But it will certainly defeat me, for it has one great quality – it is very cunning. It knows how to hide its hate under a hypocrite's mask – again a beige mask, of course – for all here is beige that can be beige, paint, carpets, curtains, upholstery, bedspreads. Everything wears this neutral mask – the village, the people, the sky, even the trees have not escaped.

But before I had half-emptied the bin I felt as tired as if I had walked fifty miles – tired and in utter despair. This bath will always be a ditch to me now and a dirty ditch at that. I was too tired to eat but went up to bed with a beer-bottle filled with hot water to keep me warm.

All the beds are cold, narrow and hard. There are three bedrooms. Photographs of Greek temples – I suppose they are temples, pillars anyway – decorate the walls of this one. There is a cheap dressing-table with a glass that won't stay put, a wardrobe to match the dressing-table and a straight-backed chair. Here too I have put bolsters along the window-sills, because I remember how well they kept out the cold in Vienna. Slowly I grow calmer, and then quite calm. I know that the second stage of loneliness is over and the bad moment is past.

Looking at the bolsters and remembering the piles of yellow-white snow and that statue of the Holy Ghost. 'Clouds in stone,' said André. 'Very German! Like the insides of a

73

turkey.' Another time he said 'The legs are the most noble, beautiful, harmonious and interesting part of the human body.' I said No, I didn't agree. We argued sitting at a table in the *Parisien* with bottles of German champagne before us. But it was not chic to drink it. Now and again you foamed up your glass with one of those wooden instruments they had and then pretended to sip. I can see us sitting there and I can see my astrakhan coat and the dress I was wearing, but it is not myself inside it. Everything is sharp, bright, clear-cut – a little smaller than life, perhaps, and the voices coming from some way off, but very clear. It is 'Rolvenden' that is behind me in the mist.

In the bedroom of the flat in the Razumoffskygasse there were low coffee tables, Bohemian glass, a big picture of Franz Josef and smaller pictures on either side of General and Madame von Marken. Pierre came in and said 'Bravo' when he saw me in my new black dress. There was a smell of lilac when you got out into the street, of lilac, of drains and of the past. Yes, that's what Vienna smelt of then . . .

2 *The Sword Dance and the Love Dance*

Every fortnight the officers of the Japanese Commission entertained their following at Sacher's Hotel. The Japanese were very dependent on their following, for not one of them could speak all three of the necessary languages – French, English, German. There were perpetual arguments over the exact translation of documents. They were afraid of not being as tactful as the representatives of an Asiatic power ought to be, or of voting with the minority instead of the majority – that would have been the end of them in Tokyo. So Colonel Hato had his secretary and confidential adviser – that was André – and Lieutenant-Colonel Matsu had his – that was Pierre. Then there were four other officers (at first -- the number increased by leaps and bounds later on), a naval attaché, the typists, who had been carefully chosen by Matsu in Paris and were all very easy on the eye though by no means all of them were efficient according to Pierre, a Hungarian interpreter, and various other hangers-on.

At the end of the long, elaborate meal some of the guests would leave and the rest of us would go into Matsu's sitting-room next door – high, silk-curtained windows, gilt furniture, shining mirrors. Then bottles of Tokay and kümmel appeared and the Japanese mask dropped. Then photographs would be produced and handed round.

'This is Madame Yoshi.'

'How pretty she is!'

'She's wearing European clothes.'

'Oh, doesn't she look smiling and happy?'

'Of course she is smiling,' Captain Yoshi said – rather grimly, I thought – 'Madame Yoshi is a most fortunate woman. Madame Yoshi *knows* that she is a most fortunate woman.'

Matsu's photographs were of his little son and of his three daughters, whose names meant Early Rising, Order and Morning Sun. He had bought them each a typewriter as a present. He never told us the son's name, or what present was destined for him. Too sacred?

Captain Oyazu had no photographs, but in next to no time he could transform the evening paper into a frog which looked as if it might start hopping at any moment, and he smiled in a pleased, childlike way when you admired it.

On this particular evening Colonel Hato and Oyazu left after the first glass of Tokay, and as soon as they had gone Yoshi began to dance.

Yoshi was the tallest, handsomest and best-dressed of the Japanese officers and he spoke French and German better than any of the others. First he danced the sword dance, using umbrellas instead of swords, and then what I suppose was a love dance, for, turning his feet out at right angles and holding an umbrella upright, he shuffled past us, looking at the women of the party very slanting-eyed and mocking.

But Simone, who was the prettiest of the typists and only eighteen years of age, answered that challenge at once. She danced opposite him with her hands on her hips, laughing, imitating exactly every step he made, and after a bit of this the strain and defiance went out of his face. He pulled her to him and began a clumsy foxtrot. André played 'Dardanella' for them on the piano.

When 'Dardanella' was finished Matsu announced, 'I will now play you a Japanese song.'

He played it with one finger, striking the notes carefully and gently, with a sad, absorbed, intent expression.

He said – he was the one who spoke English – 'That is a sleep song.'

Matsu had spent a fortnight in London and for a whole day of it he had been lost in the Inner Circle. 'When I came out it was very dark and cold. I grew frightened and sad.' (He was in London in November.)

After the lullaby he went off into a long, monotonous succession of notes, as if he were trying to make a pattern of the keys, black and white. There was music in him somewhere – he touched the piano so gently.

Yoshi and Simone were sitting at a table at the far end of the room. The others were gossiping about Hato. There was always a new story going about him. He was the one who loathed white people and said so, maintaining that contact with them would bring nothing but misfortune to Japan. He was the one who, safe in his bedroom, André said, would at once take off his European clothes, saying that they made him feel unclean, and put on a kimono and slippers with hisses of relief.

He was a small, thin man, much older than any of the others. Really very old, we thought, quite gaga. He had only one eye – he had lost the other in the Russo-Japanese War, and it had not been dolled up, either. On social occasions he would sit bolt upright, silent, staring into the distance.

'What can he be thinking of, André?'

André said, 'The poor devil is supposed to speak French. And he can't. I should say that gives him enough to think about.'

But he, too, liked music. His favourite song was 'Marjolaine'. 'Encore "Marjolaine",' he would shout. (Si gracile, si fragile . . .) 'Encore, encore "Marjolaine".'

When they had finished with Hato, Odette, another of the typists, began to tell us what she thought about Viennese clothes. She said that they were pretty but they had no real chic. 'When I went back to Paris on leave last month Maman told me, "You look like a little provincial". Maman is thirty-nine but one would say twenty-five. She cried like a Magdalene when I left – '

André interrupted, 'My God, what's happening over there?'

Yoshi was sprawled on the floor, the table and the bottle of wine were upset. He got up and brushed his clothes down, though without smiling or looking at us. André rushed forward and picked up the table and the bottle. Simone said, 'Oh, do excuse me. I'm such a clumsy girl. I've always been like that. You've no idea – the trouble I get into because – '

Soon afterwards we said good night and were out in the lilac-scented street. After we got round the first corner Simone began to laugh. She had held it in like a good one, but now it had to come out.

'How did it happen, Simone?' André said at last.

Simone said, 'I don't know how it happened. He was practising kissing the hand and I'd had enough of it and tried to pull away. He held on and crashed into the table, and down he went. I expect he'd had too much to drink. Oh, his face when he fell! Aren't they funny? And those dances with the umbrellas!'

Off she went again.

Pierre said, 'I hope he won't bear you any malice, Simone. I'd hate to be somebody the Japanese bore malice against.'

'Not he,' Simone said. 'He won't bear any malice against me, poor boy.'

None of us thought of taking cabs home that night. Perhaps there was a moon. Perhaps the streets were lovelier or more deserted than usual. Then there was that smell of lilac and of the past. Vienna still smelt very strongly of the past. We walked along, keeping rather close together.

'Well,' I said, 'he looked as if he were telling you all his secrets.'

'He was,' Simone said, 'he was. Do you know what he was saying? He was saying how much he admires the Germans. He said they'll soon have the best army in Europe, and that they'll dominate it in a few years.'

'No bouquet for the French?' André asked, laughing. 'And think how I sweat, translating their idiotic ideas into diplomatic language!'

Simone answered seriously, 'But he did say something about the French. He said the French love women too much. He said only the Germans know how to treat women. The Germans and the English think the same way about women, he said, but the French think differently. He said the English and the French together won't last another year, and that they are splitting up already.'

Pierre said, 'Oh, he's found that out, has he? Not much they don't find out.'

We walked on.

Odette said in a sullen voice, 'I'm not Anglophile, me. And why do all their songs sound like hymns?'

'I like them,' Simone said happily. 'Oh, I like some of those boys. Their clothes are so chic and they can be very nice. I like them. I like everything – everybody.' She spread her arms wide open.

'And then you wake up,' I thought.

'What beautiful enthusiasm, Simone!' said André.

Odette said, 'It's true that the English have droll ideas. The other day I was talking to Captain – You know the one, the one with the long nose and the monocle. And he said,

"I've just seen an amazingly pretty woman – " Then he stopped and went as red as fire. So out of spite I pretended I hadn't heard; I made him repeat it. "I've just seen rather an attractive *person*," he said, "in the Kärntnerstrasse." Why should he have to blush like that, when he says the word woman? Is it a dirty word in English?'

'Because he's an idiot,' Pierre said, 'and so are you a little idiot, Odette.'

'All the same,' André said, 'there's something in it. "Ma femme," you say; "Meine Frau," you say. But what would happen if you said "May I introduce my woman, Mrs Colonel?" '

'It depends on Mrs Colonel, but I shouldn't risk it,' I said.

'I used to mix up the words myself when I first learnt English,' André remarked. 'That's how I know the difference is very important. Also there's lady and girl. Very complicated.'

Of course we all knew that there were a lot of sly jokes, misunderstandings, cartoons and so on, about the British in Vienna. It was not altogether their fault – they were severely handicapped. Love affairs with Viennese girls were very much discouraged, so when they occurred they were carried on cautiously and often ended brutally. On the other hand, 'great friendships' with boys were winked at – even with the boys who at one café were to be found heavily made up and dressed in women's evening clothes. But everybody said that you ought to see them in Berlin; Vienna wasn't their home town.

André said, 'I bet if they knew in Tokyo what Yoshi told Simone there'd be trouble. They're not orthodox, these confidences.'

'No need for Tokyo,' Pierre said. 'You've only got to tell Hato. Then Yoshi would have to commit hara-kiri. Hato detests him.'

'Wouldn't that be a feather in Hato's cap?' I said.

And we all knew that not one of us would stick that feather in Hato's cap. He hated us, so we hated him – it's easy.

We had nearly reached the hotel where the girls were staying.

'Did he really say that, Simone,' asked André. 'About the English and the French splitting up, and the next war?'

'He did, I assure you,' said Simone, 'he did. He said he gave it ten to fifteen years, and after that Germany would probably dominate Europe. He said it would happen because the English and the French don't trust each other and can't stick together and that's the only thing that might stop it.'

'Ten to fifteen years is a long time,' Odette said.

'And Japan?' said Pierre. 'And beautiful Nippon? Banzai Nippon!'

'He didn't say anything about Japan,' said Simone, 'now I come to think of it. Not a word about Nippon.'

We said good night to the girls. We didn't talk for a bit. Then André said. 'The Japanese! They are not to be taken seriously. What can they possibly know about it?'

Yes, I can remember all my dresses, except the one on the chair beside me, the one I wore when I was walking on the cliffs yesterday. Yesterday – when was yesterday? ...

I had a striped taffeta dress, with velvet flowers tucked into the tight waistband. (And the waistband was round the waist, whatever the English fashion was then.) I had a white satin dress, very slick and smooth, the prettiest of the lot but the cheapest. Round the throat there were coloured stones imitating a necklace. I had a black satin dress with three flounces bordered with green, hand-sewn. With this dress I had two sashes to wear, each as elaborate as a Japanese *obi*. One was black, boned so that it made my waist look very small; the other was green, to match the borders of the flounces. I had a white muslin dress that washed like a rag, and a blue one too, made just the same. Those were my favourites. Washed and ironed like rags, they did, and always came up as fresh as daisies. I had a dirndl, and a check dress. I had a blue serge dress, the bodice fitting closely but the skirt wide and full. Its sleeves were loose, embroidered in gay colours and finished with a tassel. I had a classic English *tailleur*, but I always hated that. I had a yellow and blue dress to wear when I wanted to lie down, when I was tired. It was long and loose, the neck and sleeves bordered with blue. It was like cornfields and the sky, and looking at it made you feel happy, made you feel free. And thinking of it I am free again, knowing that nobody can stop me thinking, thinking of my dresses, of mirrors and pictures, of stones and clouds and mountains and the days that wait for you round the corner to be lived again. Riding round and round the Inner Circle, but unlike Matsu I ride knowing that it will be dark and cold when I come out, that it will be November, and that I shall be a savage person – a real Carib.

But Caribs live under different skies, by a different sea. 'They run and hide when they see anybody,' Nicholas said. Perhaps I shall do that too.

3 *Carib Quarter*

Nicholas was the overseer of Temps Perdi, an estate near the Carib Quarter. Temps Perdi is Creole patois and does not mean, poetically, lost or forgotten time, but, matter-of-factly, wasted time, lost labour. There are places which are supposed to be hostile to human beings and to know how to defend themselves. When I was a child it used to be said that this island was one of them. You are getting along fine and then a hurricane comes, or a disease of the crops that nobody can cure, and there you are – more West Indian ruins and labour lost. It has been going on for more than three hundred years – yes, it's more than three hundred years ago that somebody carved 'Temps Perdi' on a tree near by, they say.

The estate house had been empty for so long that a centipede fell out of a book when I opened it. Everything had run wild, but there was still hibiscus growing by the stone garden walls and butterflies made love over the thorny bougainvillea. Every morning Myra, Nicholas's daughter, put little earthenware bowls of fresh flowers along the low partition which separated the verandah from the sitting-room. From the verandah we could see Guadeloupe, the Saints and Marie Galante; sun on dark trees . . .

But the white-cedars at the end of the garden – the lowest about eighty feet high – had dropped their leaves and were covered with flowers, white flowers very faintly tinged with pink, so light and fragile that they fell with the first high wind and were blown away as soon as they fell. There used to be a famous Creole song about the white-cedar flowers but I can't remember it. 'Here today and gone tomorrow' – something like that, it must be.

'There is nothing to see in the Carib Quarter,' Nicholas insisted. He had a handsome Negro face, a big chest, a deep, booming voice.

'These people,' he said, 'don't even live near together. Their houses are each far away from the other, and all hidden in the bush. There is nothing to see in Salybia. Besides, the new road only goes as far as the river. After that you'll have to ride. It will take a couple of hours or so.'

'But can't it be arranged? Can't we get the horses?'

'Oh yes, it can be arranged,' Nicholas said disapprovingly.

But I wasn't so easily put off. All my life I had been curious about these people because of a book I once read, pictures I once saw.

Whenever the Caribs are talked about, which is not often, the adjective is 'decadent', though nobody knows much about them, one way or the other, or ever will now. There are only a few hundreds left in the West Indies, or in the world, and they live in the part of this island called Salybia. They have not intermarried much with the Negroes and still have smooth, black hair, small, slanting eyes, high cheekbones, copper-coloured skins. They make baskets, beautifully plaited, light and waterproof, dyed red and brown or black and white. The largest is the island's substitute for a trunk, the smallest would just hold a baby's shoe. Sometimes the baskets are made to fit one inside the other, like Chinese boxes.

Nobody else seemed to want to visit the Carib Quarter, nobody seemed at all anxious to take a long ride in the sun with nothing much to see at the end of it.

'They are supposed to have two languages. The women have a language that the men don't know. So they say.'

'They say so, do they?'

'Well, we'll ask Nicholas. ... Nicholas, isn't it true that the Carib women have a secret language?'

Nicholas said, grinning, that he thought he had heard something of the sort. Yes, he fancied he had.

Tormented with the fear that I had imagined the closely-printed book, the gaudy illustrations pored over as a child, I produced the special number of *L'Illustration*, 23 November 1935, for the *Tricentenaire des Antilles Françaises* and exhibited '*Homme Caraïbe Dessiné d'après natur par le Père Plumier*'. Early eighteenth century, probably. Bow and arrows in his right hand, a club in his left, a huge, muscular body and a strange, small, womanish face. His long, black hair was carefully parted in the middle and hung smoothly to his shoulders. But his slanting eyes, starting from their sockets, looked wild and terrified. He was more the frightened than the frightening savage.

'We had a print very like this – perhaps it was the same one – in the dining-room at home.'

'He isn't very attractive.'

'Everybody used to say that.'

And he always used to look so sad, I thought, when they laughed at him. With his wild, strained eyes and his useless bows and arrows.

'The original West Indian, is he?'

'Oh no, that's a Carib. The original West Indians were killed by the Spaniards or deported to Hispaniola – Haiti.

Well, most of the men were. The Spaniards told them they were going to Heaven. So they went. Weren't they suckers? Then the Caribs, the cannibals, came from the mainland of South America and killed off the few men who were left.'

But that book, written by an Englishman in the 1880s, said that some of the women, who had survived both Spaniards and Caribs – people were not so thorough then as they are now – had carried on the old language and traditions, handing them down from mother to daughter. This language was kept a secret from their conquerors, but the writer of the book claimed to have learned it. He said that it was Mongolian in origin, not South American. He said that it definitely established the fact that there was communication between China and what is now known as the New World. But he had a lot of imagination, that man. Wasn't there a chapter about the buried Carib treasure in La Soufrière, St Lucia – one of the mouths of Hell, they say – and another about the snake god, and another about Atlantis? Oh yes, he had a lot of imagination.

The day we went to the Carib Quarter the wind was blowing heavy luminous clouds across the sky, tormenting the thin crooked coconut-palms on the slope of the hill opposite the verandah, so different from the straight, healthy, glossy-green coconuts just round the corner of the road – tame trees, planted in rows to make copra. We arrived punctually at the place where the horses were to wait for us, but it was a long wait before they turned up, so young Charlie, aged sixteen, who was our guide, went on ahead. He was beautifully got up in white shirt, shorts and socks, but hideous, heavy black boots that squeaked with every step he took. There were stepping-stones across the shallowest part of the broad river. On one of these Charlie's horrible boots betrayed him and I thought he had fallen into the water, but he managed to save himself. When he got to the other side it was a relief to see him sit down, take off his boots and socks and hang them round his neck before he walked on.

The horses came at last. They were so thin that every bone showed in their bodies and they had the morose, obstinate expression which is the price of survival in hostile surroundings. Negroes like to be in the movement and hate anything old-fashioned, and horses are now definitely old-fashioned.

However, when we mounted they jerked their necks strongly and clip-clopped without hesitation into the clear, shallow river. I had forgotten the lovely sound of horses' hooves in water, that I hadn't heard for so many damnable years.

Then they heaved and strained us on to a wide, grassy road. There was a flamboyant tree with a few flowers out. Next month, I thought, it will be covered; next month all the flamboyant trees – the flame trees – will be covered, and the immortelles will flower, but I shan't be here to see them. I'll be on my way back to England then, I thought, and felt giddy and sick. There were a lot of iguanas along that road. I shut my eyes and saw one of the illustrations in the book about the Caribs, vivid, complete in every detail. A brown girl, crowned with flowers, a parrot on her shoulder, welcoming the Spaniards, the long-prophesied gods. Behind her the rest of the population crowded, carrying presents of fruit and flowers, but some of them very scowling and suspicious – and how right they were!

In the midst of this dream, riding through a desolate, arid, lizard-ridden country, different and set apart from the island I knew, I was still sensitive to the opinion of strangers and dreaded hostile criticism. But no, it was approved of, more or less. 'Beautiful, open, park-like country. But what an *extreme* green!'

The road had been gradually rising and, as we came round the shoulder of a hill, smiling Charlie met us, accompanied by a Negro policeman. An official welcome to Salybia? . . . Below us we saw small clearings among the low trees – low for that part of the world – and the bush riddled with narrow paths. But not a human being. ('These people live all separated from each other, and all hidden in the bush. These people hide when they see anybody.')

'That's the king's house,' the policeman announced, and I thought 'So, there's still a king, is there?'

Round another bend in the road we saw below us the big clearing where the police-station stood with five or six other houses, one of them a Catholic church.

In the station the rifles were stacked in a row, bayonets and all. The room was large, almost cool. Everything looked new and clean, and there was a circular seat round the palm tree outside.

'We had trouble here,' our policeman told us. 'They burnt the last station and they burnt twenty feet off this one while it was being built.'

'Why?'

'Well, it seems they thought they were going to have a hospital. They had asked the Government for a hospital. A petition, you know. And when they found out that the Government was giving them a police-station and not a hospital, there was trouble.'

'Serious trouble?'

'Pretty serious. They burnt the first one down, and they burnt twenty feet off this one.'

'Yes, but I mean was anybody hurt?'

'Oh no, only two or three Caribs,' he said. 'Two-three Caribs were killed.' It might have been an Englishman talking.

'There is a beautiful Carib girl,' the policeman said, 'in the house over there – the one with the red roof. Everybody goes to see her and photographs her. She and her mother will be vexed if you don't go. Give her a little present, of course. She is very beautiful but she can't walk. It's a pity, that.'

When you went in it was like all their houses. A small room, clean, the walls covered with pictures cut from newspapers and coloured cards of Virgins, saints and angels,

Star of the Sea, Refuge of the Distressed, Hope of the Afflicted, Star of the Sea again, Jesus, Mary and Joseph . . .

The girl appeared in the doorway of the dark little bedroom, posed for a moment dramatically, then dragged herself across the floor into the sun outside to be photographed, managing her useless legs with a desperate, courageous grace; she had white, lovely teeth. There she sat in the sun, brown eyes fixed on us, the long brown eyes of the Creole, not the small, black, slanting eyes of the pure Carib. And her hair, which hung to her waist and went through every shade from dark brown to copper and back again, was not a Carib's hair, either. She sat there smiling, and an assortment of brightly-coloured Virgins and saints looked down at her from the walls, smiling too. She had aquiline features, proud features. Her skin in the sun was a lovely colour.

We took a few photographs, then Charlie asked if he might take the rest. We heard his condescending voice: 'Will you turn your side face? Will you please turn your full face? *Don't* smile for this one.' ('These people are quite savage people – quite uncivilized.')

Her mother, who looked like an old Chinese woman, told us that in her youth she had lived in Martinique in service with a French family and then had been taken to Paris.

'I come back here,' she said, 'because I want to see my mother before she die. I loved my mother. Now I must stay because I am old, I am old and who will take me away?'

'She like that since she four,' she said, pointing to her daughter.

'Hélas!' she said, gesticulating. She had thin, lovely hands. 'Hélas, hélas!'

But the girl, sitting in the sun to be photographed, smiled contentedly at us, pushed a strand of hair from her shoulder to her back, smiled again. And all the Virgins and saints on the walls smiled at us too.

The night in Temps Perdi is full of things chirping and fluttering. The fireflies are out – they call them labelles. It is at night, lying caged under a mosquito-net, that you think, 'Now I am home, where the earth is sometimes red and sometimes black. Round about here it is ochre – a Carib skin. In some lights like blood, in others just pretty, like a picture postcard coloured by somebody with a child's paintbox and no imagination.'

It is at night that you know old fears, old hopes, that you know unhappiness, turning from side to side under the mosquito-net, like a prisoner in a cell full of small peepholes. Then you think of that plant with thick, fleshy leaves edged with thorns, on which some up-to-the-minute Negro has written over and over again 'Girls muck, girls muck', and other monosyllabic and elementary truths. When I was a child we used to draw hearts pierced with arrows on leaves like that and 'Z loves A'. It all comes to the same thing, probably.

But when you have drunk a good tot of rum nothing dismays you; you know the password and the Open Sesame. You drink a second; then you understand everything – the sun, the flamboyance, the girl crawling (because she could not walk) across the floor to be photographed. And the song about the white-cedar trees. 'Ma belle ka di maman-li – ' (A lot of their songs begin like that – 'My lovely girl said to her mother.') 'Why do the flowers last only a day?' the girl says. 'It's very sad. Why?' The mother says 'One day and a thousand years are the same for the Bon Dieu.' I wish I could remember it all but it is useless trying to find out because nobody sings these old songs any more.

It had a sweet sound sometimes, patois. And I can't get the words out of my mind, Temps Perdi.

Before I leave 'Rolvenden' I'll write them up – on a looking glass, perhaps. Somebody might see them who knows about the days that wait round the corner to be lived again and knows that you don't choose them, either. They choose themselves.

David Plante

For Marie Guillemin   # The Fountain Tree

She shopped, replaced cracked plates, washed the tub, dealt with bills, and, after a few months, watched his investments on which they lived.

One spring afternoon in the Boston Arboretum, she slipped into a European beech tree, the limbs of which hung to the ground, and it was as though she were in a gushing, green fountain. He followed her in, and inside, contained by the intertwining branches, the sunlight flashing on the wet leaves, everything in the world, he felt, was possible for him.

He brought the sense home with him. He sat and wrote pages and pages, which, filling and spilling, kept him free yet inside, like that tree, like Louisa.

Thinking of her, he found his pen, as if obsessed by a rarefied rhythm, evolving the possibility of her giving birth to a great wet mass of tangled flowers. One of her eyes was a moon, the other an orange.

There was no change after the birth of a baby – or, if any, it was only to relieve him of a few remaining burdens. He no longer saw relatives; they didn't object so much to his not being married as they realized not being married meant he wanted to be alone. And if friends came by less because they found James was really too much an involved husband and father, that was a relief, too. He wrote more and more, aware that somewhere in the large apartment were Louisa and the baby.

David Plante

His mind spinning, he emerged from his room one evening and found that Louisa was not at home. In the bedroom, the baby was sleeping in its crib. James Glough looked at it, touched it, and, for a second, strangely sensed it didn't belong to him. The head seemed unfamiliar and unattractive; the small clenched hands were pale. When he heard the front door slam, he went out. He met Louisa in the hall, taking off her coat.

'Where were you?' he asked.

She looked at him, a little puzzled. 'I always go out at this time to buy something for dinner,' she said. She held up a bag to him.

'Oh,' he said. He had forgotten, but she had made it no concern of his.

Louisa continued to look at him. 'Are you all right?' she asked.

'The baby looks pale,' he said.

'Of course,' she said; 'he's been colicky.'

'Oh yes,' James said.

Louisa kissed him. 'You're worried,' she said. 'But you needn't be.' She walked into the bedroom, leading with a smile, and it was as if she were leading him on to a landscape.

A month later, during the night, the baby died. It was cremated, without ceremony. James remained in the background. He didn't go to the crematorium. He stayed in his room.

But the image of the dead baby floated about his brain. Sitting at his desk, the papers piled and confused about him, he tried to concentrate on the slightly mis-shapen head, the thin neck, the fine-boned wrists and hands, but the baby, uncontrollably, swelled fantastically in flames. James got up and went out.

It was spring in Boston, just a year since Louisa had stood under that tree in the Arboretum. He wanted to go back there with her. He walked down Beacon Street to the Public

Garden. He went in and walked about, passing bright, streaked patches of flowers, looking closely at the dense trees just off the paths. He stood on the little bridge and stared down into the dim water which, all at once, appeared depthless. A little later, he returned to the apartment.

Louisa was in the bedroom, sitting on the edge of the bed. He went to her, sat beside her. She hugged him closely.

'Was it awful?' he asked.

She didn't answer.

He didn't ask her why, weeks earlier, she hadn't called a doctor. He remained silent.

But he felt closed in, gradually, by the delicate, strained attention he had to give her. He tried to work out meals, bills, cleaning. By summer, he was morose.

Then, as if overnight, she changed; she confronted him one morning with a smile so large it was almost stark. They quickly moved to the Cape, and opened the small, pine-shadowed house, shut tight all winter; the furniture, smelling of iodine, was swollen and damp. A wind billowed through the rooms.

Settled on the Cape, James returned to his writing, most of which he did on the cool, narrow screen porch. No one ever came to visit. He wanted no distractions. Whenever, unaccountably, he did feel distracted, he thought of Louisa. In the evenings, he sat on the glider with her.

She remained calm; she kissed him.

The summer burned on, the heat pressed down heavily, and Louisa quietly drifted to the beach every day after shopping. She came back to the house blacker and more beautiful each day. But James, having, he thought, created a landscape which was almost, now, self sufficient, which, like a quivering green bubble, brought him into more and more delicate reflections, wished he had a study where he wouldn't be interrupted. Louisa was careful, however: she waited till he put his pen down before she called him to supper.

On a particularly hot afternoon, unable to write, he went

down to the beach to find her. His white body appeared obscene in the sunlight, and he stared, slightly obsessed, at the pubic-like hairs about his nipples. He searched up and down the glaring beach for Louisa.

He saw her, alone, not far away, sitting under her red umbrella. He approached her, but she didn't notice, and when he came within just a few feet from her he saw her eyes were staring blankly and darkly. He stopped. He didn't know, suddenly, if he should go further. Louisa turned, but she did not appear to recognize him. James advanced and sat.

'What were you thinking?' he asked.

She smiled, as if surprised. 'Oh.' She paused, glancing about at the long white dunes, at the green sea, lost in a silence which made James imagine what she had been thinking about could only be softly hinted at. 'I was thinking that I've got to buy some sun lotion.'

'That's all?' he asked.

'I've been thinking all day about it,' she said.

'It's not important,' he said.

'It's terribly important,' she answered. She smiled again; a slightly off-centre look accompanied the smile.

'No, it isn't,' he said.

Her smile increased, but her eyes slid more to a vacant periphery. 'It is.'

James had to insist. 'No.'

Suddenly, as with a snap, her eyes focused on him as she turned quickly to him. 'Yes.'

He remained silent for a moment. He could not help himself. 'No,' he said.

She stood. Her voice jumped. 'Yes, it is.' She looked down at him, leaning a little, and walked away.

James lay back unable to think what had happened. He closed his eyes, and it seemed to him the whole beach slightly shifted. When he woke, his feet were sticking beyond the shadow of the umbrella. He sat up when he saw Louisa coming across the light-flashing sand, a little package in her hand. Her small body was sweating.

She undid the package, extracting a tube of lotion. Not resisting, he let her spread the amber cream over his shoulders and chest, and squirmed under her certain scrutiny of the hairs, moles, eruptions.

About the height of August, at the hottest part of the day, they had an argument about ice. Louisa said he should fill the ice trays with water and put them in the freezer after emptying them. He apologized, he hadn't thought of it, but, as if she had been holding back her anger over many, many similar oversights, she said: he always forgot; he'd sink if she weren't around to do all the small things he left undone. He tried to say calmly he had other things to think about.

He noticed, after, that Louisa, as though conscious greater bursts might occur, struggled against calling his attention to his leaving the refrigerator door open, to his failure to turn off the bathroom tap, to his depositing a half-eaten plum on a chair. James became equally conscious of his actions, and he resented it. But he said nothing, for there were always their nights together.

Going to sleep with Louisa was now, for him, like being freed from all the gathering stupidities of the day. He held on to her, and the feel of her loose breasts under the night gown, the damp smell from the nape of her neck, her very weight made him drop; he followed her to places all light-streaked, with large stars swimming past.

One morning, emerging from the bathroom to the porch, he found her arranging his papers on the old kitchen table he used as a desk. He stood at his distance and watched her. When it occurred to him she wasn't arranging, but looking through the loose pages, he approached.

'Is there something you want?' he asked, his voice contained.

'Yes,' she said.

He had never objected to her reading anything he wrote; he would have given her anything she wanted; but now he felt she was meddling.

'Why?' he asked, inserting himself between her and the table.

'I wondered how it was coming along?'

'Coming along for what?'

'So that you can get published.'

'I haven't any intention of getting published,' he said.

She glared at him. 'You don't?'

'No.'

'Then what are you writing all this for?'

'For you,' he said.

'But this doesn't have anything to do with me,' she answered quickly.

'It has everything to do with you.'

'No, nothing.' She suddenly seemed to lose grasp of her voice. 'You might have been describing someone else.' She pulled down her lower lids with her fingers. 'Look: they have nothing at all to do with the port holes of Spanish ships.' She lowered her hands. 'I can't find anything in all those thick pages that has anything to do with me. It's all so hideously vague.'

'Vague?' he said.

'You reread it,' she said, 'and show me where I come in. Show me, show me exactly.' She swallowed. She continued. 'You never saw the baby, either. You even didn't describe him correctly. His hands weren't humming birds' heads; his eyes weren't green bottles. You were unforgivably vague about him.'

James' voice flared. '*I* was?'

She leaned closer to him. 'Yes, *you*! *You* were!'

The second week of September, they moved back to Beacon Street. James silently, conscientiously helped her with opening the apartment, with cleaning, with stocking up groceries.

But his strained conscientiousness weighed. He started to take walks which were longer and longer each day. He walked once all the way to the Arboretum to see the Beech Tree. It was splendid: its branches hung heavy, the leaves brilliant, transparent yellow in the early fall sunlight.

To get out of the apartment after a shocking argument, James, beside himself, pleaded with her to take a drive with him. It was the middle of Indian Summer. Because he could think of no other place without associations which might lead them into a deeper struggle, they went to the Blue Hills, covered in burning red and yellow. He and Louisa walked the trails which rose and fell narrowly between slate ledges and thick, dun coloured leaves.

Their silence was tense as they walked under low branches, deeper into the woods, until, together, they stopped. The dense, aromatic woods were more silent than they, and as if filled with shadowed people listening. James reached for a stick. Bending, grasping it, standing – he felt the action took hours, and for a moment he was overwhelmingly aware of the woods about him. He looked up at Louisa, who was staring with so much pointed intensity at his withdrawal. He remained silent. Then she turned away.

'Let's go to the top of the hill,' he said.

They turned off from the trail and started up the broad side of the hill, pushing aside bushes, stumbling on outcroppings of glacier-sharp rock. They reached an area of worn bulging stones, covered with brown lichen, above the level of the trees. From the top of the hill they could see the sea and the Boston harbour to the east; the city was in front of them, blue-grey, glinting, and the gold bulb of the State House, to the left, flashed in the sunlight. To the west was a vast green flat expanse of Massachusetts. The wind caught their breaths.

James Glough looked at the gull-filled sky, to the right at the sea, then back to Boston. He felt suddenly an immeasurable desire to pick the whole landscape up, like a smooth wet stone from the ocean, and hand it to Louisa. He turned to her. The loose hair about her forehead was whipping about. She had, he thought, never looked so beautiful. But he couldn't tell her. She would turn away. He said:

'The view's wonderful from here.'

She didn't answer. He looked out again.

'You can see everything you want.'

Louisa's voice was calm, but tenaciously so. 'Not I – ' Looking at him, however, she stopped. She walked away.

He searched the rest of the hill. There were many small, tough, red-brown bushes growing from between the bald slabs of rocks. In the cracks of the stones he could see fragments of broken tonic and beer bottles, flashing green, amber, brown, blue. He wandered to the other side of the hill. He picked up a beer can and threw it into a clump of bushes. He bent down to pick pieces of glass from a small crevice in the rock. With a stick he dislodged a chunk broken from the heavy bottom of a tonic bottle: it was a very light sky blue. He closed it in his hand, and went to Louisa.

She was sitting on a round boulder in the sunlight. He held his clenched hand out to her.

'I have something,' he said.

He opened his hand.

She delicately picked the fragment of glass from his palm. She looked at him. 'What is it?'

'Hold it up,' he said.

She did; it blazed, a sudden bright blue flame, in her uplifted hand. She flung it away.

Between then and the time he left Boston, six months later, he stopped writing. Nor was he able to sleep. Night after night, he lay as on a glass plane looking down at sights beneath him: heavy, thick flowers, twisted, entangled hands, everything enlarged, all the colours disconcertingly vivid. Louisa didn't sleep either. She would turn to him and say, her hysteria held in thinly, that he had forgotten to hang his towel up after his shower, that she had found one of his ties dangling from the back of a chair. Did he expect her to do everything for him? No, he answered, no, but then perhaps he helplessly did.

One evening, at dinner, looking at Louisa staring out at

the lengthening Spring light on Beacon Street, he noticed she had a slight pock mark on the ridge of her jaw, and his mind struggled with it. But he gave it up.

He couldn't ask her to leave. It was not only that he considered the apartment hers, he wanted her to remain, he wanted to know where she was, as if he were holding her in some reserve. When he told her he would go, she screamed he must not. But he insisted. She wept all the morning of the day he left.

He had written to a brother who had a small business flat in London to ask if it was occupied, and if he could use it for a month. He implied it was to get out of an entanglement in Boston. The brother immediately sent back word that he could stay as long as he had to.

It was raining when he arrived at Heathrow, and it continued to rain for the first two weeks. James stayed in, restless. He paced the flat, turned round in corners, searched in bookshelves for magazines or books he hadn't already thumbed. He felt the more he paced about, the smaller the flat became, and the more relentless his thinking of Louisa.

He finally went out, one wet morning, for a long walk into Regent's Park over which the flat obliquely looked. The trees in the park floated, half seen, and the crocuses and daffodils were half dissolved in the misty air. He looked about trying to discern shapes. Turning cautiously around a wet, dripping bush, he thought: if there were only some new way by which he could approach Louisa . . .

He went into Regent's Park every day, and after two hours of twisting about the paths, the arbours, the dense shadowy places beneath the trees, he would find himself wondering where he was. Standing motionless, it was only when he knew he was lost, however momentarily, that it seemed to him possibilities delicately opened up. From the moments, he tried to gather the substance of a letter he might write to Louisa, which would make her expand again, which would make her large.

Bitter, one rainy day, he did not even go out to a restaurant for dinner. He switched from chair to chair. He found himself examining the room as if the furniture were Louisa, and he were violently looking for mis-shapen details. He found them, one by one; Louisa's thin mouth, her slightly crooked front tooth, and then there was the action she made, that of looking away and holding her hands out, when she accused him of forgetting something. He couldn't regret he had left. He had had to defend himself against her inexhaustible particulars. By early evening, he was mentally tired and a little sick.

He went out.

It was dark. The large black umbrella pressed down with the weight of rain and shadows. The paths in Regent's Park gleamed. The wind shook the branches. There was no one on the paths.

He deliberately turned off to walk across a great stretch of grass. The earth sank, soft under his feet. A fog rose about him, swelling over from the pond, on which he could see an island appear and disappear – a tangled, matted knot of wet vegetation submerged in the overall greyness. He thought: if he could submerge, taking any shape he wanted, and float in a space, and become a tree, a hand, a locked box, a large fish. He held to the image for a moment, then let it go. A covered body rose to his mind, in the midst of plants, and he felt himself leaning towards it.

He heard the rain hissing in the leaves.

He turned about, his brain throbbing. He thought: he must get out, and walked away quickly.

That night he tried, as if tying down little threads attached to an infinite number of small thoughts to keep them from drifting away, to write to Louisa. But it was impossible. The more he wrote, the more his awareness expanded in fantasies churning about him, and he tore his way through them. Before dawn, he threw his pen down on the heaps of crumpled papers, and went to bed.

Lying, his mind twisting about, he couldn't sleep. He tried to concentrate on Louisa. He saw her darkened blonde face. He saw her eyes. He saw her hands held about one another. He tried desperately to collect the small facts – points in the confusion he knew he must assert. He thought of her chin, he thought of her ear, he thought of the words she most often said, simply prepositions. He must hold the little points together, and, out of them, as fixing together a small solid, he must see Louisa. Then he recalled the pained, struggling expression on Louisa's face, and, right after, James Jr appeared, his own ugly baby, beating its arms and legs against its death, and he quickly rose out of bed.

He walked about the flat, anxious that he might not have left Louisa enough money, that she might be ill, that he might not have given her his address.

He wondered if he should go back immediately, and half consciously opened a drawer to pull clothes out. He stopped. He could telephone. But just the anticipation of hearing her voice made him sit on the edge of the bed to consider what she might say. Perhaps nothing.

He went to his desk, all the crumpled papers on the open flap, and dropped into a chair. He was lost in his confusion to the point of having no idea, if he should write, what would be the first word he'd use. He picked up the ballpoint, wondering, as from a great remoteness, in what sphere were the infinite, opening possibilities that would hold them? He felt his shoulder slacken. He wrote, for her:

She shopped, replaced cracked plates, washed the tub, dealt with bills, and, after a few months, watched his invest-ments, on which they lived.

One spring afternoon in the Boston Arboretum, she slip-ped into a European beech tree, the limbs of which hung to the ground, and it was as though she were in a gushing, green fountain. He followed her in, and inside, contained by the intertwining branches, the sunlight flashing on the wet leaves, everything in the world, he felt, was possible for him.

He brought the sense home with him. He sat and wrote

pages and pages, which, filling and spilling, kept him free yet inside, like that tree, like Louisa.

Thinking of her, he found his pen, as if obsessed by a rarefied rhythm, evolving the possibility of her giving birth to a great wet mass of tangled flowers. One of her eyes was a moon, the other an orange.

David Plante

The Crack

An acquaintance, about to leave for New York, rang from the airport where he had met, wandering about the terminal, a young man who had no money, nowhere to stay, and had on him a bottle of sleeping pills, which he said he would take all at once. My acquaintance hadn't known whom to call, and thought of me. I have no idea why. All we knew of one another was one grey, grainy sexual encounter, as if on a round, cold, flat plate, after which we quite simply hated one another. The acquaintance wondered if I could try to talk the young man into giving himself into the care of a clinic. He said he was Cuban. His name was Miguel. I said, yes, all right, and he put him on the phone. The Cuban had a high, lisping voice. He spoke English well. He sounded hysterical. I said that I would meet him in Harvard Square at eight o'clock.

I was five minutes early. I looked in the display windows of the department stores, looked over the clothes, books, records on sale. At ten past a policeman told me to move on. I told him I was expecting someone, and he walked away. At quarter past, I hoped Miguel would not show up, and I was angry for having agreed to meet him. I kept looking across at the M.T.A. station in the middle of the square from which he would come. I was, I imagined, standing on a thin sidewalk, and beneath it was space, smoke-filled, smelling of underarm odours, sweat and perfume, and great, horrible sheets billowed and twisted, and it seemed to me that Miguel, about to rise from the Subway, was going to come up from what I then felt, and when, finally, I saw a thin, effeminate figure walking, as if sideways, towards me, all my skin tightened. I did not want to shake his hand, but did. As we walked through the Cambridge Common and up Massachusetts Avenue, we remained silent; I did not know what to say.

He was thirty – I had expected a boy – and ugly. In the light of my living-room, he was even uglier: a long face with bulging eyes and lips, and his hair was dyed mouse-brown. He must have known how he looked, because he turned off the more glaring light. He offered no apologies. He sat, he put his hands to his face, took them away, looked at me, about the room. He said nothing.

Neither did I, but I watched him closely. His body twitched; he sat on the edge of the couch. His pants were very thin, and I could see the thighs of his crossed legs jumping beneath.

I sat back, and continued to watch him. I imagined stripping him, slowly, layer by layer, until he was stark, his long, bony, pale body convulsed about a centre of sparse pubic hair which his elbows tried to hide. I stood.

I said: 'Well.'

'What?' he asked.

'Why do you want to kill yourself?'

His face was stone hard. 'Because of a shit-head son of a bitch.'

'An American?'

'No. A Cuban refugee.'

I sat down. In the same way I wanted to expose his obscene body, I wanted to hear all the details. I crossed my legs.

'Where is he?' I asked.

'In Boston.'

'When did you last see him?'

'About three hours ago. He drove me to the airport so I

could fly back to Miami. He even bought me a ticket. I tore it up and threw it at him.'

'You live in Miami.'

'That's where my clothes are.'

'How long have you been in the States?'

'Four years.'

'Your family?'

'My parents and sister are in Havana; they can't get out.'

'I see,' I said, paused, then added: 'What do you do?'

'Now – nothing.'

'What did you do?'

'In Miami I was a waiter. In Cuba I had a career. I'm a lawyer.'

I couldn't imagine it. 'Are you hungry?' I asked.

He looked at me and tried, suddenly, to be grateful. 'I'm sorry,' he said, 'you've invited me, you've been hospitable.'

'Please,' I answered. 'I just want to know if you're hungry.'

His whole body slackened suddenly. 'Yes,' he said. I got up and went into the kitchen.

He became steadier while he ate. He told me, quite clearly, what had happened: he was in love with BiBi. The nickname made the involvement ridiculous, I thought. BiBi was all he had; BiBi was married and had a child; BiBi loved him, too, but his wife had forced him into taking psychotherapy, and the therapist, the bitch of a man, had told BiBi he must stop seeing Miguel. To make sure he did not see him, the wife had insisted that she, her son, and BiBi move to Boston. Miguel, in Miami, couldn't bear his absence; he had flown up to Boston three hideous days before with a small overnight bag, a bottle of pills, and two dollars left after the ticket. He had gone to BiBi's apartment – BiBi had secretly sent him the address – and during a birthday party for the son (the developing scene struck me as being more cynically humorous than grotesque, even if it were not, and I'm sure it was not, true), Miguel had crashed in, had gone right to BiBi, and said: 'If you don't come with me, I'll take these,' and held up the bottle. And BiBi, right then, left. They spent two nights in a hotel, and during the nights and days their love degenerated, as it had before, again and again, into that sick, push-pulling, thrashing, screaming irreconcilability they'd known since the first night they had met in a Miami queer bar three years before.

As Miguel spoke, he became more solid. He ate slowly, and finally fell into silence. After he finished eating, he yawned. I asked him if he was tired. He said, yes, he was very tired, but he didn't think he'd be able to sleep.

'Do you want to try?' I asked.

'No, no,' he said, 'I can't stay.'

'Why not? It doesn't bother me.'

He had nowhere else to go. He bowed his head when he said he would, if I didn't mind.

He undressed and got into my bed. I stayed in the living-room, tried to read, but all the while I could hear him twisting and turning in my sheets. Finally, he was silent. I read more, but read nothing. When I stood up and stretched, all my nerves screwed up. I quietly went into my bedroom, my hateful body squirming. I undressed, got into bed, lay still, breathed heavily. I pretended to fall asleep, and rolled closer to him. As with an involuntary jerk, I threw my arm about him. He moaned. I pulled him closer. He woke, but pretended he hadn't. I thought: pull away. But I peeled his pants down. His buttocks were pressed against my thighs. He was perfectly relaxed. I was trembling. His loose body, as loose as smoke, lay resigned against me. I hated him. I thought: Miguel will stay with me; will live with me; will hang on me.

The next day he said he had to go.

'Where?' I asked, straining to overcome my constraint before him. There was no reason for me to feel constrained.

'I'll go to a hotel.'

'Without money?'

'I don't need money.'

Oh yes, I understood. He'd rent a room, then take his pills. I said, blankly: 'How many pills do you have?'

'Twelve.'

'That's not enough.'

'How do you know?'

'Because I know,' I said. 'The most twelve can do is cause brain damage. You'd be an idiot, a half-rotted vegetable for the rest of your life.'

It was as though I had hit him sharply in the middle of the forehead. He sat down; he limply placed his hands between his knees.

'What shall I do?'

'Nothing.'

'Nothing?'

'You can stay here for a while.'

'No, no, I couldn't. Thank you, but I couldn't. I couldn't force myself on you. I am in a horrible state. You don't know. I talk and talk, and can't stop.' His body jumped as though a pin were suddenly stuck in his spine; he sat tensely, his hands now clenched about one another. 'I can't bear myself, can't stand myself or living or seeing or eating or talking. How could I expect anyone else to bear me?' With a frantic gesture he pulled at his hair, then let go and caved into the chair.

'Where will you go?' I asked.

'Maybe to New York,' he said quietly. 'I have a friend in New York, an American girl I knew in Cuba. I know I can call her and she'll send money for me to go, though I haven't seen her in a long while. The last time was in Cuba, six years ago. But I speak to her on the telephone often.' He seemed to be trying to recall. 'No, not often. The last time was three months ago, New Year's day. She called me in Miami. She was spending the evening alone because she wanted to. She was depressed.' He raised his hands and smiled. 'We have a lot in common, Jill and I. We're not happy.'

'Oh, happy,' I said.

Tears had begun to make wet tracks down the sides of his face. 'Yes, I know,' he said.

My voice rose in pitch. 'Does this girl in New York understand what's going on?'

'That I want to kill myself? Oh yes.'

'You've talked to her about it?'

'I had no one else.'

'What did she say?'

'She said, baby, go ahead and do it.'

I had to leave. I wanted to go quickly. I told Miguel to stay until I got back, and while I was away he could have some lunch, and call, or write, or read. I told him, touching him on the arm, to try to relax.

When I got outside, the weak image of him again burst out in a fantasy of crude sex. I was agitated, and my swollen desire pressed down.

While out, I kept thinking of this Cuban, now in my apartment, calling his girl friend, perhaps calling BiBi, too, in an attempt to pull him back, reduced to blubbering on the telephone. The more I thought of Miguel and his involvement, the angrier I became. But my anger was inordinate. None of my emotions, I think, had anything to do with the pin-pointed situations and people I chose as explanations. And now my exaggerated anger had taken the shape of Miguel, and Miguel, bloated by anger, became, in the course of two hours, immense enough to possess me. I walked back up Massachusetts Avenue with the desire to break him.

I was worked up when I opened the door and walked in. I didn't know if I would slap him, or perhaps bring him to the floor, or violently hug him and ask him, with a tone of supplication that implied straps, to forgive me. I hadn't had breakfast. My stomach was light and floated somewhere in my chest. Miguel was lying on the couch as though asleep. I approached him, my books in my hand, and stood tensely over him, waiting. He opened his eyes, looked at me, then closed them.

My voice was stiff. 'Are you all right?' I asked.
He nodded his head yes.
'What happened?'
He didn't move.
'Did you call your friend in New York?'
He nodded again.
'And?'
His face, which was remarkably impassive, split down the middle and two halves twisted against one another. He opened his mouth, and his voice broke out. 'Oh, she's dead!'

Miguel did stay with me – for two weeks. I fed him. I told him not to worry about money. He slept a great deal, or sat in the living-room reading magazines. I hired a television set for him. Sometimes, in the evening, he would go to the Brattle, or even into Boston, for a movie. He cooked, cleaned, made the beds. I told him to think of simple things, like furniture, like soap operas. But he was not interested. There was only one topic, really, that preoccupied him, for if he thought about it as much as he talked about it to me, he didn't have time to think of anything else: this was Jill. Jill developed, enlarged, became dense, and, sometimes when I came home and found the living-room filled with smoke, and Miguel sitting, doing nothing, I had a feeling that this girl had been there and left just before I returned.

I won't try to duplicate everything Miguel said about her. I'm sure his elaborations grew into fictions; she could not have been that beautiful, that warm, that sensitive. Nevertheless, with increasing pressure, she held the air in my apartment. She opened doors, stood in closets, made water unexpectedly run from the tap.

I began to dislike her. The complications about her were enormous. Miguel indulged himself in her, he said he should follow her, and I felt he was forcing her on me. As the days passed, he became more and more animated, and I became less.

And then, about ten days after he had first come to my apartment, the telephone, as it so seldom did, rang, and a voice asked for Miguel. Miguel spoke in Spanish. After he hung up, he said nothing, and I flared.

'Who was that?' I asked.

'BiBi.'

'Have you been seeing him?'

'I saw him once.'

'Where?'

'I'm sorry. I didn't want to concern you. You've already taken more from me than anyone else would bear for two minutes.'

'Where?' I insisted.

'Here,' he answered, perhaps wondering why I should be so offended. I wanted to know if they had made love.

'When?'

'Yesterday.'

'What did you do?'

'We talked. We're trying to reconcile. I'll be reasonable – '

'I don't know what kind of crap you're feeding yourself,' I broke in. 'It isn't going to work.'

'Yes, it will.'

'Of course it won't. You're the kind of person nothing works for.'

'How do you know?'

'Look at you: you don't have the strength to support a hair.'

'What?' he asked.

'Never mind,' I said. 'I'm just telling you it would be less hard on you if you realized now – '

'That I can't ever get up from this flat, horrible position?' he interrupted me.

'You won't,' I said. 'You'll lie there.'

He looked at me. 'Is that what you want?'

I turned away. 'Well, go, if you're going.'

'May I stay a few more days?' he asked. 'It will take that long for BiBi to get an apartment.'

I turned back to him. 'Can't you call him something other than BiBi? The name's a joke.'

He didn't answer.

I stood still. 'Stay as long as you like,' I said.

I never found out if he made love with BiBi in my apartment, and when he left I grovelled in my bed as for a scent of their bodies, for a hair. I went down with a hoard of fantasies, fantasies that undid me, so that I became lost in smoke, lost in sweat, lost in chairs, in bottles, in trees. I would not be saved. I wanted to die. I, I, I wanted to die – nobody, not Miguel, not even Jill, nobody wanted as much as I. If death were a devil, I would have conjured him up, would have crawled into his bowels to rot there.

Five days after he left, Miguel called. He said he and BiBi were giving a party, and would I come? I said yes.

They had taken an apartment on Beacon Street in Boston, not far from the Public Garden. If Miguel had no money, BiBi must have had enough. The apartment was big, and filled with over-heavy furniture: big oak Spanish chests, taller-than-a-man candleholders, paintings with baroque frames, red plush, wrought-iron grilles. I wondered if this had all been brought from Cuba or bought here. It was a sustained, obvious attempt to re-create in furniture an atmosphere that must have been familiar to these people in their own country. The well-made-up girls were in high fashion, Miguel wore a dark tailored suit, BiBi wore a velvet smoking jacket. His wife was there. I noticed a few non-Cubans: some boys I had seen in the bars, a girl I knew was a whore.

Miguel was light-headed. He kissed me on both cheeks. He took me about and introduced me to everyone, assuring me in a loud voice that they would like me; they had to, as I was so kind it showed. He was intolerable.

I talked – or tried to talk – with BiBi. He thanked me for helping Miguel. I said: 'It was natural, really.'

'What?'

'Well, one doesn't want other people to die.'

He laughed. 'I'm not sure. I've seen a lot of it.'

He was bigger than I, and towered, leaning, over me. I easily saw him in khaki and army fatigue clothes, a rifle slung on his shoulder; he even had the soldier's grimace. Yet he fitted, too, in the black velour jacket.

Miguel came up to us; I wondered if he was concerned we might become too friendly. He said: 'I hope you get along.'

'Oh yes,' I said.

'I thanked Joseph for helping you,' BiBi said.

'He did help, tremendously,' Miguel said, then turned to BiBi and smiled, and BiBi, smiling stupidly back at him, ran his hand through his hair.

I said nothing. When they both turned away, I took my coat and went out, burning, my anger like a tense surface holding me together.

I imagined Miguel and BiBi day and night. I would sometimes wake at night from dreams in which they, arm in arm, laughed at me idiotically. I began to think they had used me, and my hatred for them grew wild. I imagined whipping them, pounding them with nails, beating them with boards.

And then, as I should have expected, Miguel called shortly after, on a Sunday evening, his voice tight and low. He said BiBi had thrown him out three days before, and he had been wandering since then, staying up all night, sleeping like a bum in the Boston Public Library during the day. He did not ask if he could come; he waited for me to offer. My first impulse was to tell him to go to hell, but, after a horrible pause, I told him to get into a taxi and come; I would pay.

He talked, like an alcoholic, until dawn about BiBi, and as the room got ashen, he slipped into talking about Jill. I gave him something to eat, something to drink, hoping food would settle him, but he talked on and on, until a kind of rhythm had come into his voice, a rhythm like twanging strings. He repeated and repeated, he talked around and around, the words BiBi, BiBi, Jill, Jill, Jill, hit little drums, and finally Jill, pill, Jill, pill were beaten on one great big drum which had no direct sound, but a cavernous resonance. Miguel was in a state I had never seen anyone in: he might as well have been dead, for he looked calm and distant. His evolving talk, or devolving talk, reached wider and wider peripheries. I did not see in him enough personality for me to even describe him as a black pit. He was not even that. And yet he talked, talked while the sun rose, talked while our beards grew, talked while cars started in the garage next door, while people passed and talked among themselves, and he seemed to change shape, to grow spines, to flatten, to swell out, to become small almost to vanishing, and once I thought he got on all fours and jumped beneath the couch from where he stuck his head out and squealed at me. And then, I don't know when, like some thin grey grainy lava, he began to spread out, to fill the room, advancing towards me, and what amazed me, what I was aware of all the time, was that I made no effort to draw back.

But he stopped just short of touching me. He had finally let go; he had fallen asleep. I don't know when he did fall; it seemed to me he had been asleep while he spoke those last two hours in which he mumbled, repeated, circled, broke off, began again, his voice declining. His head was against the couch; his mouth was open, and he was drooling. I got up, pulled the blinds, and wondered if I should wake him and put him to bed. My mind spun.

I still had the cord of the blinds in my hand. It weighed like lead, and the texture felt enormously rough and uneven. The pale light behind the blinds blazed through the slits, so I had to close my eyes, and in that moment, in the time it takes for a crack to appear, I saw, through the crack, an incalculable distance, and heard, distinct, precise, clear, arching the distance like the fine, fine tail of a white comet, my own voice calling me. It called again, from so far, from such remoteness, from I would never know where.

I turned; he was sitting upright, still, numb, looking at me. I wanted to run up to him, grab his thin neck in my hands and break it; I wanted to be in a high place so I could throw him off; I wanted to crush him. But there again, calling, was that voice. I was not sure any longer that it was mine. And then, the crack in me opened wider, and I fell open, and I filled, spilled, overflowed, fountained, gushing, and running out and out. There he was, still sitting, lost, perhaps not even wondering what I would do to him. I didn't like him, I didn't have anything in common with him. I had no idea what to do with him. He looked about, he raised his hands and put them on top of his head, he breathed in, he pleaded:

'Joseph – '

And I, breathing out, breaking on table edges and chairs, falling, sinking, seeping away, thought: 'You'll help him.'

Three years later he left for Mexico City.

Bernard Malamud

My Son
the Murderer

He wakes to a feeling his father is in the hallway, listening. Listening to what? Listening to him sleep and dream. To him get up and fumble for his pants. To him not going to the kitchen to eat. Staring with shut eyes in the mirror. Sitting an hour on the toilet. Flipping the pages of a book he can't read. To his rage, anguish, loneliness. The father stands in the hall. The son hears him listen.

My son the stranger, he tells me nothing.

I open the door and see my father in the hall.

Why are you standing there, why don't you go to work?

I took my vacation in the winter instead of the summer like I usually do.

What the hell for if you spend it in this dark smelly hallway watching my every move. Guessing what you don't see. Why are you spying on me?

My father goes to his room and after a while comes out in the hallway again, listening.

I hear him sometimes in his room but he don't talk to me and I don't know what's what. It's a terrible feeling for a father. Maybe someday he'll write me a nice letter, My dear father . . .

My dear son Harry, open up your door.

My son the prisoner.

My wife leaves in the morning to be with my married daughter who is having her fourth child. The mother cooks and cleans for her and takes care of the children. My daughter is having a bad pregnancy, with high blood pressure, and is in bed most of the time. My wife is gone all day. She knows something is wrong with Harry. Since he graduated college last summer he is nervous, alone, in his own thoughts. If you talk to him, half the time he yells. He reads the papers, smokes, stays in his room. Once in a while he goes for a walk.

How was the walk, Harry?

A walk.

My wife told him to go look for work and a few times he went, but when he got some kind of offer he didn't take the job.

It's not that I don't want to work. It's that I feel bad.

Why do you feel bad?

I feel what I feel. I feel what is.

Is it your health, sonny? Maybe you ought to go to a doctor?

Don't call me by that name. It's not my health. Whatever it is I don't want to talk about it. The work wasn't the kind I want.

So take something temporary in the meantime, she said.

He starts to yell. Everything is temporary. Why should I add more to what is already temporary? My guts feel temporary. The world is temporary. On top of that I don't want temporary work. I want the opposite of temporary, but where do you look for it? Where do you find it?

My father temporarily listens in the kitchen.

My temporary son.

She said I'd feel better if I work. I deny it. I'm twenty-two, since last December, a college graduate and you know where you can stick that. At night I watch the news broadcasts. I watch the war from day to day. It's a large war on a small screen. I sometimes lean over and touch the war with the flat of my hand. I'm waiting for my hand to die.

My son with the dead hand.

I expect to be drafted any day but it doesn't bother me so

much any more. I won't go. I'll go to Canada or somewhere, though the idea is a burden to me.

The way he is frightens my wife and she is glad to go off to my daughter's house in the morning to take care of the three children. I'm left alone, but he don't talk to me.

You ought to call up Harry and talk to him, my wife says to my daughter.

I will sometime, but don't forget there's nine years' difference between our ages. I think he thinks of me as another mother around and one is enough. I used to like him, but it's hard to deal with a person who won't reciprocate.

She's got high blood pressure. I think she's afraid to call.

I took two weeks off from work. I'm a clerk at the stamps window in the Post Office. I told the superintendent I wasn't feeling so good, which is no lie, and he said I should take sick leave, but I said I wasn't that sick. I told my friend Moe Berk I was staying out because Harry had me worried.

I know what you mean, Leo. I got my own worries and anxieties about my kids. If you have two girls growing up you got hostages to fortune. Still in all, we got to live. Will you come to poker Friday night? Don't deprive yourself of a good form of relaxation.

I'll see how I feel by then, how it's coming. I can't promise.

Try to come. These things all pass away. If it looks better to you, come on over. Even if it don't look so good, come on over anyway because it might relieve the tension and worry that you're under. It's not good for your heart at your age if you carry that much worry around.

This is the worst kind of worry. If I worry about myself I know what the worry is. What I mean, there's no mystery. I can say to myself, Leo, you're a fool, stop worrying over nothing – over what, a few bucks? Over my health that always stood up pretty good although I've had my ups and downs? Over that I'm now close to sixty and not getting any younger? Everybody that don't die by age fifty-nine gets to be sixty. You can't beat time if it's crawling after you. But if the worry is about somebody else, that's the worst kind.

That's the real worry because if he won't tell you, you can't get inside the other person and find out why. You don't know where's the switch to turn off. All you can do is worry more.

So I wait in the hallway.

Harry, don't worry about the war.

Don't tell me what to worry about.

Harry, your father loves you. When you were a little boy, every night when I came home you used to run to me. I picked you up and lifted you to the ceiling. You liked to touch it with your small hand.

I don't want to hear about that any more. It's the very thing I don't want to hear about. I don't want to hear about when I was a child.

Harry, we live like strangers. All I'm saying is I remember better days. I remember when we weren't afraid to show we loved each other.

He says nothing.

Let me cook you an egg.

I don't want an egg. It's the last thing in the world I want.

So what do you want?

He put his coat on. He pulled his hat off the clothes tree and went downstairs into the street. Harry walked along Ocean Parkway in his long coat and creased brown hat. He knew his father was following him and it filled him with rage.

He didn't turn around. He walked at a fast pace up the broad avenue. In the old days there was a bridle path at the side of the walk where the concrete bicycle path was now. And there were fewer trees now, their black branches cutting the sunless sky. At the corner of Avenue X, just about where you begin to smell Coney Island, he crossed over and began to walk home. He pretended not to see his father cross over, although he was still infuriated. The father crossed over and followed his son home. When he got to the house he figured Harry was already upstairs. He was in his room with the door shut. Whatever he did in his room he was already doing.

Leo took out his key and opened the mailbox. There were three letters. He looked to see if one of them was, by any chance, from his son to him. My dear father, let me explain myself. The reason I act as I do is. . . . But there was no such letter. One of the letters was from the Post Office Clerks Benevolent Society, which he put in his coat pocket. He brought it up to his son's room, knocked on the door and waited.

He waited for a while.

To the boy's grunt he said, There is a draft board letter for you. He turned the knob and entered the room. Harry was lying on the bed with his eyes shut.

You can leave it on the table.

Why don't you open it? Do you want me to open it for you?

No, I don't want you to open it. Leave it on the table. I know what's in it.

What's in it?

That's my business.

The father left it on the table.

The other letter to his son he took into the kitchen, shut the door and boiled up some water in a kettle. He thought he would read it quickly and then seal it carefully with a little paste so that none leaked over the edge of the flap, then go downstairs and put it back in the mailbox. His wife would take it out with her key when she returned from their daughter's house and bring it up to Harry.

The father read the letter. It was a short letter from a girl. The girl said Harry had borrowed two of her books more than six months ago and since she valued them highly she would like him to send them back to her. Could he do that as soon as possible so that she wouldn't have to write again?

As Leo was reading the girl's letter Harry came into the kitchen and when he saw the surprised and guilty look on his father's face, he tore the letter out of his hands.

I ought to kill you the way you spy on me.

Leo turned away, looking out of the small kitchen window

into the dark apartment-house courtyard. His face was a mottled red, his eyes dull, and he felt sick.

Harry read the letter at a glance and tore it up. He then tore up the envelope marked personal.

If you do this again don't be surprised if I kill you. I'm sick of you spying on me.

Harry left the house.

Leo went into his room and looked around. He looked in the dresser drawers and found nothing unusual. On the desk by the window was a paper Harry had written on. It said: Dear Edith, why don't you go fuck yourself? If you write another such letter I'll murder you.

The father got his hat and coat and left the house. He ran for a while, running then walking, until he saw Harry on the other side of the street. He followed him a half block behind.

He followed Harry to Coney Island Avenue and was in time to see him board a trolleybus going towards the Island. Leo had to wait for the next bus. He thought of taking a taxi and following the bus, but no taxi came by. The next bus came by fifteen minutes later and he took it all the way to the Island. It was February and Coney Island was cold and deserted. There were few cars on Surf Avenue and few people on the streets. It looked like snow. Leo walked on the boardwalk, amid snow flurries, looking for his son. The grey sunless beaches were empty. The hot-dog stands, shooting galleries, and bathhouses were shuttered up. The gun-metal ocean, moving like melted lead, looked freezing. There was a wind off the water and it worked its way into his clothes so that he shivered as he walked. The wind white-capped the leaden waves and the slow surf broke on the deserted beaches with a quiet roar.

He walked in the blow almost to Sea Gate, searching for his son, and then walked back. On his way towards Brighton he saw a man on the beach standing in the foaming surf. Leo went down the boardwalk stairs and on to the ribbed-sand beach. The man on the shore was Harry standing in water up to his ankles.

Leo ran to his son. Harry, it was my mistake, excuse me. I'm sorry I opened your letter.

Harry did not turn. He stayed in the water, his eyes on the leaden waves.

Harry, I'm frightened. Tell me what's the matter. My son, have mercy on me.

It's not my kind of world, Harry thought. It fills me with terror.

He said nothing.

A blast of wind lifted his father's hat off his head and carried it away over the beach. It looked as if it were going to land in the surf but then the wind blew it towards the boardwalk, rolling like a wheel along the ground. Leo chased after his hat. He chased it one way, then another, then towards the water. The wind blew the hat against his legs and he caught it. He pulled the freezing hat down tight on his head until it bent his ears. By now he was crying. Breathless, he wiped his eyes with icy fingers and returned to his son at the edge of the water.

He is a lonely man. This is the type he is, Leo thought. He will always be lonely.

My son who became a lonely man.

Harry, what can I say to you? All I can say to you is who says life is easy? Since when? It wasn't for me and it isn't for you. It's life, what more can I say? But if a person don't want to live what can he do if he's dead? If he doesn't want to live maybe he deserves to die.

Come home, Harry, he said. It's cold here. You'll catch a cold with your feet in the water.

Harry stood motionless and after a while his father left. As he was leaving, the wind plucked his hat off his head and sent it rolling along the sand.

My father stands in the hallway. I catch him reading my letter. He follows me at a distance in the street. We meet at the edge of the water. He is running after his hat.

My son stands with his feet in the ocean.

Biographical Notes

William Sansom

born 1912 in London, is one of the most consistent of contemporary short story writers, both in the quantity of his output (he has published over twenty-five titles including ten collections of short stories) and in the quality of his writing. He was a frequent contributor to *Penguin New Writing* during the war and the last volume (1950) included a story by him. His appearance in the first volume of *Penguin Modern Stories* marks a link with an illustrous predecessor.

Jean Rhys

born in 1894 in Domenica, West Indies, suffered eclipse for many years after a brilliant career in the twenties and thirties with her short stories *Left Bank* and her novels *Voyage In The Dark* (1934) and *Good Morning Midnight* (1939). Ford Madox Ford said of her work: 'She combines an almost lurid passion for stating the case of the underdog with a singular instinct for form.' Late in the 1950s she broke her long silence with some new short stories *Tigers are Better Looking* and a new novel *Wide Sargasso Sea,* published in 1966. This brought her acclaim and the W. H. Smith Award, and she is once again among the most valued of contemporary writers.

David Plante

born 1940 in Providence, Rhode Island, U.S.A. is a full-time writer who has four novels in his desk drawer. The fifth entitled *Slides* is soon to be published, and he is currently working on the sixth.

Bernard Malamud

born in Brooklyn in 1914, has written five novels, *The Natural*, *The Assistant*, *A New Life*, *The Fixer* and *Pictures of Fidelman*. A master of the short story, his collections include *The Magic Barrel* (which won the National Book Award for fiction in 1959), and *Idiots First*.

More about Penguins

Penguinews, which appears every month, contains details of all the new books issued by Penguins as they are published. From time to time it is supplemented by *Penguins in Print* – a complete list of all our available titles. (There are well over three thousand of these.)

A specimen copy of *Penguinews* will be sent to you free on request, and you can become a subscriber for the price of the postage – 4s. for a year's issues (including the complete lists). Just write to Dept EP, Penguin Books Ltd, Harmondsworth, Middlesex, enclosing a cheque or postal order, and your name will be added to the mailing list.

Some other books published by Penguins are described on the following pages.

Note: *Penguinews* and *Penguins in Print* are not available in the U.S.A. or Canada

Short stories by Bernard Malamud

Idiots First

The distinctive Malamud flavour –
brilliant – nutty – sad

Still Life. A frenzied comedy of an American artist's
attempts to seduce the woman who shares his studio in
Rome.

Naked Nude. Forced by art thieves to fake a Titian, the hero
of *Still Life* finds he prefers his forgery to the original –
so he steals it himself . . .

The Cost of Living. A heart-rending account of the agonies
of a poor Jewish grocer when a chain-store supermarket
opens up next door.

A Choice of Profession. A few dealings with an experienced
girl student decide a cuckold-turned-teacher to look yet
again for the right choice of profession.

Idiots First. The story of a poor Jew trying to raise money
for his idiot son's train journey to an aged uncle in San
Francisco.

The Assistant

To be poor is bad enough; to be a poor Jew is a crime.
Frankie Alpine should have known that a Gentile
should never try to help a poor Jew and he brought
tragedy to the house of Morris and Ida Bober.

A novel of a writer now recognized as one of the most
powerful talents on the American literary scene,
twice winner of the National Book Award.

Not for sale in the U.S.A. or Canada

The Fixer

Bernard Malamud

'A novel that offers a great experience, first of all a literary experience, but not merely that' – *Saturday Review*

Kiev, in the years before the First World War, is a hot-bed of anti-semitism. When a twelve-year-old Russian boy is found stabbed to death, his body drained of blood, the accusation of ritual murder is made against the Jews. Yakov Bok, a handyman, is blamed, arrested, and imprisoned without indictment. What becomes of this man under pressure, to whom acquittal is made to seem as terrifying as conviction, is the subject of this outstanding novel.

Also available
The Magic Barrel
The Natural
A New Life

Not for sale in the U.S.A. or Canada

Wide Sargasso Sea

Winner of the W. H. Smith and Son Literary Award for 1967

Jean Rhys

Jean Rhys's first novel since 1939, the most amazing literary reappearance of our time, *Wide Sargasso Sea* is the story of the first Mrs Rochester, the mad wife in Charlotte Brontë's *Jane Eyre*.

Antoinette Cosway is a Creole heiress; product of an inbred, decadent, expatriate community; a sensitive girl at once beguiled and repelled by the lush Jamaican landscape. Soon after her marriage to Rochester, rumours of madness in the Cosway family poison Rochester's mind against her; Antoinette's beautiful face turns 'blank hating moonstruck' . . . and the action narrows, as inexorable as Greek tragedy, towards the attic in Thornfield Hall, the grim Grace Poole and the suicidal holocaust of leaping flames.

Voyage in the Dark

A chorus girl of eighteen in a fit-up touring company, Anna Morgan sees England as a succession of identical cold hard towns, greyly contrasting with the flaming colours of her West Indian childhood.

A brief liaison with a kindly but unimaginative man leads Anna to abandon the theatre and drift into the demi-monde of 1914 London: red-plush dinners in private rooms 'up West'; ragtime, champagne and whisky back at the flat; these, and a discreet tinkle of sovereigns in the small hours pave the way to disaster . . .

First published in 1934, Jean Rhys's account of Anna's fall from innocence was far ahead of its time.

Not for sale in the U.S.A.

Good Morning, Midnight

Jean Rhys

Back in Paris for 'a quiet, sane fortnight', Sasha Jensen
has just been rescued by a friend from drinking
herself to death in a Bloomsbury bed-sitter.

Despite a transformation act, new clothes and blonde
cendré hair dye, Sasha still feels 'not quite as good
as new'. Streets, shops and bars vividly evoke her
Paris past: feckless husband Enno, baby born dead,
sundry humiliations in abject jobs . . .

One night, a gigolo mistakes Sasha for a rich woman –
she still has her fur coat – and their subsequent liaison
somehow distils the essence of all that has gone before.

Not for sale in the U.S.A.